The Time Traveller

RAY WILLS

(The Gypsy Poet)

Copyright © 2021 Ray Wills

All rights reserved, including the right to reproduce this book, or portions thereof in any form. No part of this text may be reproduced, transmitted, downloaded, decompiled, reverse engineered, or stored, in any form or introduced into any information storage and retrieval system, in any form or by any means, whether electronic or mechanical without the express written permission of the author.

This is a work of fiction. Names and characters are the product of the author's imagination and any resemblance to actual persons, living or dead, is entirely coincidental.

ISBN: 9798719040585

CONTENTS

ABOUT THE AUTHOR

ACKNOWLEDGEMENTS

CHAPTER ONE: THE TRAVELLING MUSH

CHAPTER TWO: AFFAIRS OF LITTLE EGYPT

CHAPTER THREE: KINGSBERE FAIR

CHAPTER FOUR: MARY FANCEY

CHAPTER FIVE: CHILDHOOD DAYS

CHAPTER SIX: UPON THE DOWNS

CHAPTER SEVEN: THE HEATHER LANDS

CHAPTER EIGHT: TURBARY RIGHTS

CHAPTER NINE: CAMPFIRE NIGHTS

CHAPTER TEN: GYPSY DIPS AND DALES

CHAPTER ELEVEN: BENEATH LODGE HILLS

CHAPTER TWELVE: GENTLEMENS AFFAIRS

CHAPTER THIRTEEN: GYPSIES AROUND THE YOG

CHAPTER FOURTEEN: THE SQUARE AND THE COMPASS

CHAPTER FIFTEEN: THE OLD PURBECK ROUTE

CHAPTER SIXTEEN: HEATHER VIEW

CHAPTER SEVENTEEN: TRAVELLING DAYS

CHAPTER EIGHTEEN: REFLECTIONS

GLOSSARY

SOURCES AND RESOURCES

ABOUT THE AUTHOR

Ray Wills was born in Newtown Poole Dorset in 1945. Rays childhood and early youth was spent in Dorset on the Mannings heathland Poole Next door to the Poole councils Gypsy traveller encampment. Then later at Wareham. After leaving school at Kemp Welch Parkstone Poole. His first job was as a painter and chassis sprayer for Bluebird Caravans the largest caravan industry in the world. Than as an Officers Batman in Bovington Dorset before joining Community Service Volunteers.

Ray worked closely with the National Playing Fields Association for many decades. Establishing and managing numerous children's adventure playgrounds and play projects throughout the UK in inner cities and rural communities.

Ray has been a member of numerous poetry groups in Dorset and is a social historian and an authority on the history of the Gypsy community. His qualifications include a Royal Society of Arts Diploma in Management and Senior Youth worker City and Guilds certificate. At present he lives within a community of artists, writers and musicians in the village of Bere Regis in Dorset. Here he continues to give talks on local history and poetry readings throughout Dorset. Ray is project co ordinator of Kushti Bok the Gypsy traveller welfare organisation. He works closely with both Poole and Dorchester Museums and the Dorchester Heritage centre. He operates numerous community organisation pages on Facebook.

His previous publications have included "The Gypsy Storyteller" anthology for Francis Boutle Publisher, "Romance in the Everglades" poetry anthology- published by xpress publications. "The Canford Chronicles "a poetry Anthology, "Where the River Bends", "Adventures in Child's Play" "The Gypsy Camp" and "Gypsy Tales". He writes numerous articles for magazines including the "Traveller Times" and "Play and Playground".

THE TRAVELLER

He had travelled those fairgrounds
and all those great shows and fares
he'd shod a few horses and he'd sold of his wares
his buck-boards and tackle and all his attire
for to ride on the switch backs with a welcoming smile

Oh the life it was hard then but the people were free
for to travel those lanes through the open country
where there's birdsong each morning and starlight at night
through the furze and the bracken
it was Gods great delight

The people were rich then in their culture and lore
they talked of their histories and their flights and the wars
though they rode on their vardos and bent benders a few
amongst the hills of Scotland and the harbour of Poole
all the stories were told around their yog fires anew
where their chavvies did chatter and the old ones brewed stew

Where their chores were a plenty and the songs they were sung
of Caroline Hughes and the rabbits did run
yet only the farmers blessed the roar of the guns

Ray Wills

ACKNOWLEDGEMENTS

The Author is indebted for the support and material provided along with permission to include extracts from discussions in interviews. I am grateful for the following people who assisted me with this book. Mrs Jean Hope Matthews.

For reading my drafts and giving me lots of technical advice and encouragement throughout Brian Cordell, Susan Miller and Lizzie Crouch for providing me with permission to use the front cover picture.

CHAPTER ONE

THE TRAVELLING MUSH

THE TRAVELLING MUSH
I travelled down the highways
down those Gypsy lanes
talked with squires and farmers
pat the horses mane

I strolled across the meadows
to the Gypsy site
the blossoms were a buzzing
the sun was high in sky
we sat around the yog that night

We talked just you and I
the stories that we shared that night
of times so long ago
fairground Gypsy boxers
the winds the frost the snow

The mushes that we knew and loved
the gypsy girl and I
the lovers that we hugged loved and more
the fishes in the streams
the lost horizons in the mist
the long forgotten dreams

The shadows and the sunsets
the chavvies running free
the lovers on the meadows sweet
all past histories
yet seemed so real to me

The thunder storms and rainfall sweet
the horses and the rides
the fairgrounds and the weddings
the suitors and the brides

The vardo wheels a turning
the wheelwrights Coopers frames
the Stanley with the handsome bricks
the chaffinch down the lanes

The running brooks and meadows
the haystack where we lay
sweet corn rising on the distance
I hear a cry a new baby born
welcome to the morn

Ray Wills

Cinderella Rose Lee

Cinderella the Gypsy lived upon the great South Shore
where the Blackpool Golden mile stretched
and was well worth waiting for

They called her Rose Lee
for she was a seer and true
she told you lots of fortune tales
on the beach at old Blackpool

Her booth it was well lit up with pictures by the score
close by the donkeys serenades upon the Blackpool shore
she wore a scarf of gaiety and her lamp it was well lit
her cards spread on the table just across from where's you sit

Her eyes they looked right into you like she read your mind and soul
she was dark and beautiful and her rings she did fare show
her dress was long and dignified like a lady of good taste
her skin was dark and mystical and her beauty in her face

Of all the Gypsy ladies her words were true to form
she told you how it was from the day that you were born
her booth no longer sits there on Blackpool's golden mile
where lads and lassies came to call to see her golden smile

Ray Wills

Fairground Tales

She read it in his tea leaves
before the starlight show
there beneath the canopy
of the wonder fairground show

He heard her words of mystery
for Gypsies cannot lie
she read it in his palm that day
before the crowds went by

Within the sounds of the Children's laughter
all of the loud melodic rock
Bill Haley and the comets
Elvis and the rolling stones on trot

Now Gypsies cannot lie
she looked into her crystal ball
looked into his eyes
her scarf and golden earrings
her rings and tattooed arm
she used all her Gypsy charm

He wondered how she knew so much
it could not all be lies
she promised love and fortune soon
a lovely summer bride

He was transformed by her ways
her intuition and her styles
She read it in the night time skies
within the wondrous show
a fairground rich in wonders
hers was a Gypsy wonder show

Ray Wills

"Living-vans of-green. and gold with their flapping canvas covers; domed tents whose blankets of red and grey had faded at the touch of sun and wind; boarded porches and outgrowths of a fantastic -. character, the work of Romany carpenters; unabashed advertisements announcing Gypsy queens patronised by-duchesses and lords; bevies of black-eyed, wheedling witches eager to pounce upon the. stroller into Gypsydom; and troops of fine children, shock-headed and jolly"- Revd George Hall.

This South Shore encampment had existed from 1836 when Ned and Sarah Boswell first arrived here.Its members have included the Lees,Boswells,Herons,Youngs,Townsends   Smiths.Robinsons, Petulengros and Townsends. When I came here today the Gypsy fortune teller caravan's were still being visited regularly by famous celebrities. The Petulengro Roma family were still working the cards in their booths like they had done for generations. Amongst Lords and ladies and celebrities from all over the world Epsom was well known as the headquarters of all those Gypsy families.

I looked around at all the attractions here with my friends. We were all out for the day, maybe pull some chicks, if were lucky. Here there were entertainers, acrobats, stilt walkers and men with their three-card or thimble-rigging tricks. The sands still attracted all the Lancashire holiday-maker's in their thousands from all areas of the UK. With its shooting-galleries, merry-go-round's, switchback ride's, water chute's, and other side shows and Gypsy horse sales. Children particularly loved the organ-grinders here, not so much for the music but for the monkey which almost always accompanied them. The children who were here were so eager to feed the monkeys that it is doubtful that the man ever had to spend much on food for them. There were women organ-grinders too they usually had a cage of budgerigars. If you paid a penny, a bird would pick out from a drawer beneath the cage a printed card that would tell your fortune. It was always something pleasant and written in such a way that it could apply to almost anyone. These people wore rings in their ears, brightly coloured scarves and swarthy complexions; many were Italians. Sometimes they were accompanied by a dancing girl playing a tambourine, which she would also use as a tray to collect money.

Who would have believed me when i would relate these happenings later. This my first visit to Madame Rosa booth . I saw the large billboard outside of her booth. It read Madame Rosa gypsy fortune teller to the stars. I entered her booth for my teenage mates having dared me earlier. And Who was I to not to take a dare.

I knocked on her door and then entered her dark booth which was lit only by a kerosene lamp. She sat facing me and was dressed in a floral colourful outfit of cottons and silk. She was sat at the table, cards in her hands as she gestured for me to take the seat facing her. Her headscarf was just as colourful as I had expected. She wore bright gold ear rings dangling from her small ears. Her eyes were so dark, pretty blue and mysterious. I couldn't help but noticing that her dress top was open and so revealing some cleavage. I was attracted to the sight of top of her breasts and felt slightly uncomfortable at the sight of her beauty. I stared at her and felt her eyes looking deeply into mine. As if she was reading my very thoughts. I took the coin from my tight jeans pocket and placed it in her outstretched hand. Then she took it from me putting it aside. Then she asked me. " So you you want a palm reading" I replied "yes". She smiled at me and took my right hand holding it gently in her own feminine hand,her soft fingers stroking my palm. As she looked intently at me and then at my hand. Then she looked deeply into my eyes. Then after what seemed like a lifetime she spoke. "You are a traveller" "You have a strong lifeline, you will have much love and very many women will desire you". "You have a deep need to travel". "Though yours will be travels in time, for you have the sign". I looked at her into her eyes and was mesmerised, barely able to take in what she said. My eyes tried not to stare at her low cleavage, her breasts so revealing. She saw my looks smiled at me and said "You have the sign of the rose tattoo." She pointed to the point above my left eye at my birth mark. She once again repeated herself. "You have the sign"she said "The sign of the rose tattoo." I didn't know what she was on about. Only that her eyes were so so desirable. She spoke again softly as she touched my forehead. "You are blessed with great wisdom and you will travel in time." She spoke again "You will see much and learn a great deal and your wisdom will be profound." I felt uncomfortable as if she was looking into my very soul. She spoke again. "You will find much love wherever you go and you will uncover great secrets of your people." She said "As you leave my booth today you will travel in time." "You will be lifted, spirited away." "You will see and experience much.". "You will be educated in the arts and have intuitive powers of greatness." She spoke again"You will have intuitive powers, with the ability to foretell things and events." Then she smiled at me again and said "That's it." "Kushti Bok my Raymond." "Good bye" I said "Kushti Bok".

I was shocked that she knew my name as I hadn't told her. Then I hurriedly left her booth and was out in the bright daylight outside. I felt weird and shaken and it didn't help when I looked for my young friends and they didn't appear to be anywhere. Plus the fact that everything around me all looked so very different outside now. Different than from earlier before I had entered her booth. The fairground was still here but it had changed considerably, its billboard names and the rides were now all was so different. I made my way towards where the bus stop was earlier. But even it was now nowhere to be seen.

I thought over what Madame Rosa had said. "You have intuitive powers with the ability to foretell things and events."

I knew that she was right of course, as i always could tell the exact time day or night without a watch. I had many times had those intuitions. The feeling that's something was happening amongst my friends or family before they confirmed it had. I also had strange colourful dreams every night and sometimes I witnessed events in my dreams. Events that happened, occurred exactly as in my dream shortly after. Such as a plane crash, a political or world event /situation or the death of or illness of someone close to me. Regularly I had hunches not to go somewhere or they'd be trouble. Sometimes I took notice, or someone persuaded me to do something against the hunch, it usually was a girl. As a result I met many problems. And it caused me to question if they were the right one for me. I knew that I was easily led by my emotions, my feelings. And as a result I fell in love so easily. How it was that I would hear something about someone then uncannily I would bump into that very person who had been in my thoughts. Meeting them by chance in the street. Often it was someone I had not seen for years. Or I was told of a death and it was like deja vu. I knew what the person would be saying exactly before they spoke. Before the words came out of their very mouth. Yes I had the gift I thought, but in many ways for me as a young man it was a curse. As for me being able to travel in time. That's a bit weird I thought.

It all seemed to be like a dream today and it was also so strange. What was even more strange was the fact that the booths and fairground looked so different from when I had arrived here earlier today. And where the hell did my young mates go to. As I realised they too were still nowhere to be seen. I didn't feel right. I felt tired emotionally drained and I sat down on the nearest seat. Which was in fact the bottom wooden step of a small Romany vardo gypsy wagon which was unattended and with no horse. Although as I discovered later the wagon actually had a plaque on the side which read Madam Rosa dream wagon.

I looked inside the wagon through the small window and saw the bed, it looked so inviting to me. There was no one around it was quiet here and as usual I followed my intuition. Slipping inside the wagon and as I stretched out on the soft feather down mattress I straight away fell fast asleep and I dreamt.

CHAPTER TWO

AFFAIRS OF LITTLE EGYPT

Our Little Egypt Race

In times of Knights Templar
Richard Lionheart and the Turks
In our community shanty town
by the remote seaport

We lived a life of simplicity with families and kin
we entertained the holy pilgrims
and allotted for our sins

We danced we sang and entertained
wth our fancy clothes and trinkets we held the reins
we entertained the pilgrims from the holy lands again

We were a gysy tavelling race
we worked in sun and rains
so proud of all our skills
smithery and games

In our little Egypst sanctuary on the great highway
we are a race of gypsy grace
afore we left our homeland space
to seek our freedoms on the distant plains

Ray Wills

Lords of Little Egypt

They were lords of Little Egypt
they rode across the plains
youl nevr see their likes again
they camped outside the cities
with their loyal gypsy bands

All the greatest performers dancers
singers to
craftsmen of the bricks and potteries

They were Roma kings and Princes
with the fortune telling knaves
beautifull young ladies
dressed like indian braves

They never had no bible
but they knew the lord of hosts
they sat aroud the yog at night
mushrooms on their toast

Kings and Queens they welcomed them
the Pope he gave his best
stories they could tell a few
like all were heaven blessed

Ray Wills

Intuitive Gypsy Roma

The third eyes intuition dictates
the fortune tellers contemplates
insightful precise origins of the east
like cards of wisdoms readings and bells on feet

Tents of drapes and occult themes
wisdoms stories myths and mankinds dreams
the oracle and the eyes of themes
the gaze and looks into the stars unseen

The dark mysterious worlds of wonders and faith
tattoos and songs all rich in tome
nomadic lives of indian homes
the past and the future in one look

Wise and rich in history in the book
insightful wisdoms love of the craft
stepped into the future from out of the past

Ray Wills

Royal Blood

Royal blood running through their veins
misplaced forgotten race here they go again
golden silver pots and pans donkeys mules misplaced man
trinkets and prophecies in biblical sets
casanove lovers violas accordians and castanets

Kings and queens counts and dames
caravan peoples black and free biblical names
Soloman and Lev histories
Persian cloth and silk from the east
christian teachings and roma speech

Place those cards and rioll that dice
fortune and story tellers in the night
crowns and paupers entourage free
papal letter seeking sanctuary

In Rome with the Pope holy lands pilgrims eloped
Turkish warriors swords and shame
gypsy bretheren know their names
penances and christian oaths
noble men escorts in bridal bethrothes
seeking truth and liberties
brother band across the seas

Ray Wills

I awoke from a deep sleep the vardo dream wagon was in complete darkness. I stumbled around in the dark eventually finding my way to the lantern and the box of swan vestas matches. I struck the match and the vardo lit up.though what i saw in the light starled me.for i was not in the vardo. I was in a far different place it was a place the likes of which i had never known. All around me high on the walls were coloured bulbs all lit up. From above the high walls of the room hung long drapes of numerous colours. The flooring was of a large oriental Persian carpet. Then i saw him there in the far corner he sat faceing me. He was cross legged his arms were folded and he was stareing at me intently. He was wearing clothes of which i had never seen the likes of before except in old pictures of the Arabian Knights. His headdress was that of a shiek, consisting of a turban decorated with fine jewells and his clothes were those of an Arabic or Persian nature."You look worried sir" he said in a rich orient or arabic accent which i didnt recognise. "Where am I", i asked "how did i get here." He replied."One question at a time master" "First of all the place wherin we live is known to all our people as Little Egypt. I am called Prince Rupert of the fells.." "We are travellers of the orient and this is our homeland".I looked around astonished and asked him again "How did i get here/" He replied" Why, through time and space of course, for you are indeed a time traveller gypsy". Then he got up from his position on the floor and said". "Come follow me." I reluctantly followed him being unsure of just where he was taking me. I followed him through a long heavy red drape into another room. This room was much larger and grandier. It had numerous grand framed art pictures on its walls which were of gypsy camps, horses and beautifull half naked women. Many of the pictures of the women were in provocative positions proudly showing off all of their nakedness.Around the room were many gold furnishings and fancy coloured cushions. At the far end was a grand table where sat two fine looking gentlemen. Both of whom were dressed in robes and uniforms of a kingly nature. They both got up from their seats as I entered and beckoned for me to sit by them at the table.They introduced themselves. The taller of the two spoke "I am Duke Andrew and this is my younger brother Michael" "We are both returned from the holy lands". "Welcome to Little

Egypt" he said and offered me his hand and a kiss on the cheek. His younger brother did the same. He then beckoned to me, "Sit down my brother" he said. I sat down in the chair, which despite its hard appearance was a lot more comfortable than i expected. The elder Prince said "Kushti". Which surprised me as i was not expecting such a common gypsy word, especially not from a foreign Prince. He said "We have met with his holyness the Holy Pope", "Yes we have "said the younger Prince Andrew, excitedkly, beaming all over his face. "And we have the papers from the Pope signed by himself, which give us rights to travel throughout the kingdom". Then Prince Michael said "We have 100s of our peoples assembled here". "They are all from the many tribes of travellers who will come with us". "To seek refuge and hospitality amongst all christian nations of the kingdom". I nodded my head knowing a little about these first travellers from the place known as "Little Egypt: But I had never actually discovered whether such a place actually existed or was just myth. Then Prince Micheal said to me, "Ah before we talk more our guest may like some wine and to partake of some food with us" "Yes" i replied " That would be very nice."

Then he stood up from his chair and clapped his hands. Upon which a short bald headed bare topped man entered the room and said "Yes master". Prince Michael smiled at him and said, "Bring us and our guest good wine and the finest dishes". "Yes Master" the man said and hurriedy left the room.Shortly after he returned with a bottle of red wine with glasses on a silver tray. Then Prince Micheal poured the wine into the three glasses handed the glasses to me and his brother then made the toast. "Heres to success of the Gypsy travellers", "May they all have good fortune, bountiful lifes with beautiful fertile women lovers in their beds" ," Amen" said his brother and i smiled.

After a shared food offering of oysters and other delicacies followed by grapes and melons i thanked my new aquaintances. They told me a little about their times with the Pope and then Prince Michael said "We will shortly be on our pilgrimage worldwide". He then gave a hand gesture for me to walk with him and said"Now we would like to introduce you to our people at our encampment Little Egypt". When i stepped outside into the hot sunlight i was totally astonished at the sight before me. The terrain was of sand desert lands full of tents for as far as the eye could see. Tents of all descriptions sizes and colours. Yet scattered and thronged around them were a multitude of peoples. For it was a tented city. Prine Michael turned to me and said "Welcome to Little Egypt".The people were dressed in a range of clothing some richy attired and many in rags.They were of many races many dark others fair and the noise was deafening. Throughout this encampment were small fires not unlike the yogs i knew. Where sat groups of families busy eating and sharing their Says. I turned to Michael and said "This is amazing". Prince Michael asked me "Would you like to meet some of your brothers and sisters of the road". "Yes" i answered. He led me aside to the rear of a large marquee and there before my eyes was a caravan of camels. Here there were hundreds of travellers in line stretched out into the distance as far as the eye could see. Prince Michael gestured to a tall eldely woman gypsy to come forward. As she approached i was surprised to her likeness to Madam Rosa the fortune teller from Blackpool. Then prince Michael spoke to her and introduced me to her. "Annabella this is a traveller from the future can you tell him a little about your work". The lady was dressed in a black silk dress, thin and comfortable and she wore gold ear rings. Her hair was braided and dark, dark as her complexion,she looked to be around 70 years of age but she may have been much older. She smiled at me and spoke." I am Annabella i am a teacher of the occult i guide others to thruths from times past and to the future". "I use tarot, my intuition, palm readings, i ching and tea reading". "I teach our people to use their own intuitive powers i am of all faiths and of none". She then said to me"These folks are leaders many of true Romany blood and some are of royal blood". "They are Kings, Queens, princes and princeses, I teach them all great arts of the orient"."Let me introduce you to some of them." I followed her as she walked down the line of folki. Then she stopped before a handsome man and said,"This is Solomon he is of the Standley tribe, a leader and great warrior his people are great workers of iron". This gypsy stood tall with large shoulders i recognised his features. He nodded to me and said "good day Mush" i replied "good day my friend". Annabella stopped by another ,this time a prety young girl."This is Brittania Smith shes from a tribe well versed in Dukkerin and the men in her tribe in Smithery". Britania smiled at me and nodded her greeting. As we moved down the long line of gypsies i was aware that Annabella was very selective whom she chose to introduce to me.then she stopped where two men stood together side by side these were both much darker than the others."This is James King his people are entertainers skilled in the great arts of shows and this is his cousin George Castle they are basket makers and also show people".Both men were of very dark complexions as i expected just like my own family also shy and they nodded. Annabella continued her introductions. This time a short stocky man who looked very strong. " This gentleman is Crusoe Bozell he is expert with horses and donkeys". Annabella continued to take me down the long line of these people. Introducing them to me one by one. As she did so, giving me some background to their skills. So it was that I met the many tribe leaders whose characteristics and skills had never changed throughout the years and generations. Then i was introduced by her to a well groomed figure of a man. Smart in appeareance with a look of nobility. Annabella smiled and said to me ."And This is Gideon Fancey he is a skilled brick maker and has much knowledge". I shook hands with Gideon and as i looked into his light blue eyes i saw and recognised the likeness to my great grandmother Emily Elizabeth Fancy.

Annabella turned to me and said "Thats the end for today my friend. I hope you found that interesting" "You see our people are all rich in character, skills and insightfull". Then from inside her long veil dress she produced an item which appeared to be a large heavy book." This is for you" she said "it will assist you on your journey". I took the book from her and thanked her. The book was old, thick and heavy. I thanked her once again. Then she said "Theres no need to thank me the book will be of great benefit to you in your travels" "I shall now take you back to Prince Michael I expect that yould like to freshen up and rest before you go on your journey". "Yes thank you so much",i said "its been a real insight for me".

I was feeling tired but i wondered what she meant, before i go on my journey. We walked back to the large tent where the prince greeted us. He greeted me "Welcome welcome" he said, using his hands in a Persian gesture. "I hope that you found your visit to our people most valuable and insightfull." he said."Yes" i answered "very much so Sir". The Prince then led me back into the centre of the tent. He turned to me and said "We have your travell vehicle brought here for you" "where you can rest before your journey my friend". He then embraced me and kissed my cheek "Salom" he said "God be with you."

Inside the large tent in the far corner was my vardo dream wagon. I took my book into the vardo and laid it on the bed. Then i heard the voice of Prince Rupert of the Fells who had originally escorted me. He said " If youl be so kind master please follow me and you can freshen up"

"Pease help yourself master." I followed him into another room where there were light enamalled and gold bowls with many bars of exquisite colored perfumed soaps and the towels of wools of all colours. Each bowl had perfumed warm water, I chose a pink bowl and a yellow soap and washed my face and hands then later the prince escorted me back to the vardo. He said,"Have a good journey master many blessings" he gestured rolling his hands and departed. I laid on my bed and held the book in my hands. Its pages were thick with lots of scriptural references. Its title was of large print THE TIME TRAVELLERS ALMANACK. The front page cover and throughout were full of well painted pictures of a vast variety of symbols and pictures. These included those of the square and the compass, a pyramid, sheafes of corn, an all seeing eye, a tattoo of a rose, a vardo wagon,a bender, a tent, a yog fire, a deck of cards, the sun and the moon, bunch of fruit, hops, a gypsy fortune teller, a circus showman, a fairground big wheel, a pugalist boxer,darts, a goldfinch,a rabbit, a steam enginea cand a crystal ball.

I turned the pages and began to read its chapters. All were written in italic script of olde world. The headings of each read like a bible. Its chapters included, THE ROSE TATTOO, THE SAYS OF THE YOG, THE NAILS OF THE CROSS, THE JOURNEYS, THE TWELVE INSIGHTS, INTUITIVE DREAM MAKERS,

THE THIRD EYE, THE PATHWAY TO ENLIGHTMENT, THE PILGRIMAGE and THE WONDERFULL BLESSINGS. I knew that i had somthing very special in my hands.

I slipped the book under my pillow and fell fast asleep and dreamt.

CHAPTER THREE

KINGSBERE FAIR

Upon Woodbury Hill

Once Gypsies camped on Woodbury hill
it were the home of fairs
and folks remember it still
with fortune telling booths and village gal's
olé in the tooth along with blacksmiths tending hooves

Where Hardy penned and folks did boast
he shot at the famous fairground galleries most
for as Hardy said Bere it were a blinkering place
where thousands came to this kingly place

Since way back in the 12th century
they sold ponies there and gathered sum
on the hill of Hardy's green afore the sun
there were thin men and fat ones ladies too
miles away from the port of Poole

With two headed calves,dancers and performers alike
locals charged for Grokels to park their bikes
with coconut shies and nine pin stalls
lots of fun for girl and boy

It was held each September for a week
where folks did travel across from Dorchester streets
As well as faraway places such as Birmingham,Bristol Exeter and
also all the Cockney chums
with oyster day and penny day too

It boasted it was the biggest in the south
those days are gone and the hill still stands so proud
with woodland copses and green pleasant grounds
lording over this little town

Ray Wills

The View from the hill

There once was a brewery
with its meads and its butts
in the village of Bere
with its cress fields and streams
its lovely rich countryside
where poets once d dream.

There once was a Barnes family
who lived by their skills
building neat houses
amongst wagon wheels.

In country rich farmlands
and hillsides a few close by old Shitterton
its bridges leas and views

The yokels did tell
of the Durberville courts
the old landed gentry
the Drax and the Kings
the kingly of sports

All the dray horse
afore the dawn did awake some
in the first days of spring.

You can feel it today
as you walk amongst pastures anew
and look down
to May's fine plantations
oh what a view.

Ray Wills
Gypsies I knew
I once knew a Gypsy
he had him a farm

he raised sixteen children
with a gal on each arm

He loved all the ladies
he had so much charm
he rode him a wagon
and he sang him a song
I once knew a Gypsy
with curls in her hair
such a beautiful body
made the boys stare

She sang like a bird
and she went to the fairs
she told them their fortunes
the wise men and fools to beware

She took all their money
their hearts and their souls
then she skipped down the lanes
where nobody knows
I once knew a Gypsy
they called him the great Gypsy king
he bred him the goldfinch
oh how they could sing

They said he could barter
never lost any deals
he lived upon whisky
fermented in stills
I once knew a Gypsy
now I never lie
he had him a brickyard
chimney as tall as the sky

He made him some bricks there
some red and some white
he sold them abroad

then sailed out of sight
I once knew a Gypsy
tall stories he told
such amazing stories
like Gypsies of old

He took him a wife
then he took him some more
he lived on the heather
out there on the moors
I will tell you no more

Ray Wills

It was early morning when I was awoken from my deep sleep by the sounds of bird song. I could feel the movement of the vardo wagon wheels beneath me in the night and the sound of the horses hooves. Hear the sound of the whip and the driver swearing. But I knew there was no driver of this Romani vardo dream wagon now I opened my eyes and found my way outside but all i could see were the leafy branches of tall trees overhead. The landscape was very familiar to me. I recalled when as a child I had regularly caught the little single decker bus to this place from Wareham. And at another occasion in my youth i had played in a football game in one of the dung infested undulating meadows in the village. From my easterly position on the high ground above the village. I looked down to the scene below and i recognised the church far below in the village itself. At least that has not changed i thought. As I stood up on the highest point above the village. A place known to the locals as Woodbury hill and I yawned and stretched my legs. Then I looked across and out in the far distance i saw the Rye hill and the farmyard. Then to the right the high ground of the black hill in the far distance. I saw the furrowed meadows stretching out across the undulating land watched the horse at work pulling the plough in the fields.

The village streets below were busy with horses and carts and folks on push bike. I was aware that there was no heavy motor traffic to be seen now. Hardly any noise apart from cartwheels and bicycle bells. The people all seemed to be dressed in Edwardian clothes. The men wore cloth caps and sported moustaches and the women all wore long ankle length dresses and pretty ribboned bonnets. The garage on the hill which was familiar to me with its pumps was no longer there. All of the cottages all seemed to be of thatch roofs now and not the familiar tiles I remembered. I wondered if the Barnes brothers builders ancestors had built these cottages. The Royal Oak and the Drax Inns buildings were still there and there was another public house in the distance called the Greyhound. I watched the postman stop in west street. It looked like there was a post office I saw him enter inside it. The bridge and the village stream were still there with its water so clear. And far out in the distance I could just see the other bridge at Shitterton. Which was over the Bere stream which was as I recalled always full of young trout. Though now both of the bridges were both of wooden and stone construction. I could just make out a small willow tree beside the Shitterton lane bridge. I looked around at the high wooded land around me with its panoramic view. Then I saw the postman again on his crude bicycle and his bag hanging over his shoulder cycling the narrow lanes of the village. Then my thoughts were interrupted as i heard voices close by. Though these were of a rich Dorset dialect a dialect which I had not heard the likes of since childhood. When i had been on the quay at Wareham and the local farmers gathered at midday on market days. Notably Millser Green, old Charlie Samways along with old man Charlie House and his daft son Freddie. Then my thoughts were interrupted as a very attractive blue eyed and fair haired young woman approached me. She was wearing a delightful ribboned white bonnet on her head and she wore a thin cotton white long flowing dress. A dress which reached down to her ankles and showed of her figure. She saw my admiring looks then smiled at me and asked."Be you staying for the fair mister sir." "We baint seen ee here afore mister sir." "Your not of those parts be you" she asked. Whilst she gave me a strange look gazing at my appearance. Staring at my open top blue striped shirt with its high collar and then down at my light blue tight wrangler denim jeans. I must have looked very strange to her I thought.

    I smiled at her, then said. "No I am just visiting." "but id sure like to see the fair miss."

    She replied. "Well you, you will have to come back this afternoon then Sir." "For it baint bee starting till then you." "It l be in the clearing, through there see." She pointed through the trees.

    I looked to where she pointed and saw a large flat area of ground which went way back. Within its expanse it was full of caravans, fairground rides and booths. As I looked I couldn't help but notice the large sign there displayed in bold letters which read "BARTLETTS FAIRGROUNDS." Then the girl turned towards me and asked,"Would You like me to look after your bike mister, then you can collect it when you go and You will know it will be safe." I replied "Yeh that's kind of you." She smiled at me and I thought to myself that she's obviously attracted by my youthfulness and fascinated by my strange appearance. What with me in jeans and high collared shirt I must look so out of place here. "Its very hot today" I said."Yes it do be very hot the sun be very bright here." she said. She spoke again in her broad Dorset accent. "That will be cost you though Sir." "That be three pennies". "Yes of course" i said as I took the money out of my tight jeans pocket. "That's it there" i said, pointing to my modern Raleigh bike. A style and appearance that she obviously found most fascinating. She took my change from my out stretched hand and then straight a ways went over to my bike and admired it. Then she looked back at me and said, "It sure looks very different, baint it, that's for sure" and laughed out loudly. "But I will look afore it,for you Sir."

    Then she proceeded to walk away pushing my bike into the yard in the front of her cottage to the rear of the woodland. I watched her leave. Then as she walked away I couldn't help but notice how delightfully attractive she was. Such a shapely young woman I thought. Then as if it was a blessing, (a gift from the Gods) the hot suns rays shone directly upon her. It shone intensely and penetrating onto and into the rear of her thin white cotton dress. In so doing revealing her shapely partly naked body within the dress. Leaving little to my own imagination. Showing off the contours of the rear of her bottoms cheeks of her semi naked body within the dress as she walked. She was beautiful I thought as I delighted in my view of her body as she walked away. Then she turned her head and looked back directly at me and gave me a shy lovely knowing smile. As if she knew, aware that I had been admiring her shapely figure within her dress. Then she smiled at me again and blushed. Her eyes lighting up her face, as she called back to me. "You can get it back e'er later tonight sir" "afore the fair ends when it be dark",I assumed that she was referring to my bike. "il leave a light on in my porch for ya she said.." "Just knock the door Knocker." " I be Mary."she said "That be my name."

    Then as she went into the woodlands she looked back at me and once again gave me that look. As if it was that of a promise. Then she waved at me and shouted out "Bye." And then she was gone, but not forgotten.

    Throughout that morning I watched the comings and goings of the visitors from my high position on the hill. As hordes of gypsy travellers arrived in their vans and horse drawn wagons. With many putting up their tents and creating their benders in a nearby field close to the fairground. I recognised their familiar family builds and ways and knew that many of these were in fact from another gypsy site. Probably the nearby one at Gallows hill on the Bere road, which i had obviously passed on my ways here. I thought to myself that these families could well be from the tribes of Does,Penfolds, Jeff's, Greens, Blands, Burdens and Hughes.

Then by the early afternoon all of the roads and lanes all around the village were thronged with people.Their goods, horses,wagons and livestock all heading their way up here to the fair. The crowds had greatly increased in number by the late afternoon. Untill it looked like the whole of the village was but a mass of people of all shapes and sizes. I wandered around the fairground site watching the workers preparing the rides and stalls. Then to the right in the distance i saw the gypsy encampment. It was full of crude benders and poor mens canvass tents and sacking. There were a few of the gypsies around which i recognised the look of. Such as the Kings and the Coles with their familiar dark tanned skins. Just then i was tapped on the shoulder by a tall broad shouldered chested man. He wore a fancy gold waistcoat,tweed jacket, dark brown trouser bottoms and heavy boots. He also sported a large handle bar moustache which made him look rather important and distinguished."You looking for somthing mush" he asked treatenengly.

"No " i answerered. Then he spoke again "Well you best bugger off then mush, before they sees ya noising around."

I looked at his face and his dark moustach and his stare. It was the look of the gypsy eye. I had seen that look before. "Yes mister" i answered and proceeded to walk away both from him the clearing and further back into the fairground site. It was then that I saw and got into lengthy conversation with a local young man. From his fine appearance I guess that he was around 28 years of age and quite affluent for the times. A gentleman no doubt. He sported a rather long beard with a distinguished trimmed moustache and well groomed hair. Whilst his shirt, coat, waistcoat and trousers were all of good quality. He told me that he was something of an expert on gypsies and fairgrounds. He went on to tell me that he was a local photographer. He introduced himself as John White Bosville. His very name giving away his gypsy ancestral blood. He told me all about the origins of the Bere fair and all the fairground gypsies. He showed me some of his photographic work. These including a lovely photo of the mill owners the Scutt family at the local Chamberlaynes mill. It was interesting that the elder man of the group in the photo was proudly showing off a large fancy birdcage with canaries.

John Bosville said "The fairs been here since the 13th century the season finished in November around Bonfire Night"he said "that was when they settled for winter preferably on family-owned land, or where the landowner was sympathetic".

He said "The women gypsy repaired and made clothing and aprons and the men repaired and painted sideshows and stalls like 'knock 'em downs', shooting galleries and 'gallopers.' (horses)." "They devised new attractions".

"You see" he said, "fairgrounds are one of the first places one can see 'cinematographs,or have a photo taken".

He then went on to tell me "It was gypsies who sourced and purchased 'swag'. (traveller term for prizes – coconuts were especially popular).

Then he took out a magazine from his bag. It was a crumpled up copy of "The World's Fair" and obviously well read. "This is the showman's magazine" he said. He handed it to me and said "Take a look at them Sir,you an keep that one I have others." "Thanks" I said.

Then I looked through its page where all manner of novelties were displayed, it included large pink jugs at 10 shilling a gross and 'Special Large Glazed Tall Figures' at 9 shillings a gross.

He went on to tell me that "Today's traders at the Bere fair." (Which he told me proudly was "The biggest fair in the whole of England) "

He said that "people came from as far afield as Birmingham, Norwich, Bristol, Exeter and London" "As well as all over areas of the county and beyond."

He went on to tell me "Many of the local gypsies worked for local farmer's on their estates here , fruit picking and potato gathering" "Whilst others are in trading or bartering their many skills such as sharpening knives and making pegs, floral presentation's or wreath's."

I thanked him for sharing all of his knowledge with me. I told him " Its been nice to meet you John I found it all most interesting". But I did not tell him or let on, that I knew most of it anyway. I then went on my way towards the attractions in the fairground. As I wanted to see what the fair was like for myself and try my luck at the darts and coco nut shies.

After trying my hand on the coco nut shies and darts without success. I bought myself a sandwich from one of the nearby village girls sellers of refreshments. Along with a tankard of ale from a publican from the village Inn, who had set himself up in a tall heavy canvas tent. I was surprised by the freshness and the sweet taste of the pickle and ham. I saw that the villagers who lived on the hill were all busy selling refreshments from their yards. Whilst many others were very busy charging for bike parking facilities.

The sun was high in the sky and it was still extremely hot for an autumn day. I chatted for a while with some of the traders of horses and watched them bartering. I was amazed by their handshake deals. Them spitting on their hands before they shook hands smacking hard on the deal. Obviously a man's word means everything these days.

By the evening the place was jam packed with people this was particularly so once the fair had begun. There were children of all ages mixing in the crowds most of them with their parents. Some were noisy and excited squealing with pleasure at all the many attractions. Many children crowded onto the rides and carousels with their gay horses and the music was deafening. I heard folks say that the nearby town of Dorchester was deserted today like a ghost town. Amongst the people present I noticed the neat appearance of the famed writer local poet Thomas Hardy. It was obvious that on reaching the summit here he was in his element. Quite a number of local farmers, dealers and frequenters of the fair seemed to know Hardy well

I noticed that very soon he was into deep conversation with a large group of them. Then later the word had obviously got around that Hardy was present and crowds gathered to watch him at the shooting galleries. He was a crack shot with the gun and proved himself so by winning many prizes. I noticed he gave these to the local girls. There was no doubt he had a sharp eye for both the gallery and also for the local young ladies. I noticed that he was quick to flirt with some attractive young village girls too. He obviously knew many of them well and it was obvious that they were not slow in responding to his cheeky advances. Kissing him on the cheek and cheekily giggling.

The fair itself was no doubt the largest of its kind in the whole of the south of England. Just like the local photographer guy John Bosville had said. For it contained a multitude of booths and stalls. There were many scattered homes of the performers and dancers nearby at the rear of the site. There were large signs advertising thin men, fat women,two headed calves a two headed sheep and a bearded lady. Plus there were gayly colored china ornaments on display. I noticed that the nut brown Gypsy women fortune tellers booths were all crowded out with local village girls. All no doubt seeking to have their fortunes told and to find a man to marry or to run off with to foreign shores. The noise from the crowds was deafening. As the showmen shouted out above the noise of the crowd and sold their wares. Whilst all the dancing gypsies girls played castanets on into the night.

I noticed two tall young men busy shoeing two horses at the rear of the fairground. I wandered over and watched them at their work. Admiring their physical strength, their muscular appearance and their skill with the horses. They told me they lived locally and were in fact brick yard workers at their Amey family brickyard at nearby Doddington. They told me that there were in fact 3 brickyards in Bere Regis which provided work for locals as well as those of gypsy descent.Their two white cob horses were strong very well cared for and obviously the pride of their family. Very neccesary for transporting bricks and heavy work at their brickyards. The Amey brothers told me that the horses were called Ginger and Nobby.

Then as the air got colder i looked at my watch and saw that it was ways past nine thirty. I decided that as the fair was nearly over for today. I thought it was time to go in search of my raleigh bicycle and Mary the village girl with the sparkling blue eyes, fair hair and other hidden delights. I said farewell to the Amey lads and left them. Then i went through the fairground site past the stalls and made my way ot into the dark wodlands and the cottages.

CHAPTER FOUR

MARY FANCEY

Saturday nights and Sunday mornings
I had never had cider with Rosie
or slept naked out under the stars
upon a grassy hillside with heather on my back
But Mary from the dairy had changed all that

I had never watched the stars at night
or lost myself studying the milky way
I had never played with butter cups spread out
or laid daisies on her naked form
on a silver chain of loveliness
where love was truly born

I counted all my blessings then
as i lost my sinful shame
how did it happen
I guess Mary was to blame

She took me in the night
before the morning dew
I lost my virgin birth to her
but she saved me from myself I guess
and I was born anew

Ray Wills

Rye Farm

I walked to Rye farm upon top of Rye hill
where chickens did peck and ganders ran still
where goats they did chew from the leaves of the bush
and i sat down for breakfast with another wise mush
had ate fresh laid eggs and the bacon so good
the farmer he served me the best that he could

The turkeys were calling and the dogs they did yap
i ate of my toast crumbs on my lap
there were cows in the fields at the back of he sheds
the road it was busy with tanks full of lead

The countryside spread was a sight to be seen
just like Hardy wrote oh delightful of scenes
the farmer was Crocker the free loving man
he raced all the dogs at Poole racing stands

The walkers and tourists they often called
I sat with the yokels, the grockers and all
It was warm in the summer on top of rye hill
where the farm it was rich in manure smell still
where the poets told stories and of Cyril wood fame
from the village of Bere and top of Butt lane

There was Bloxworth and Shitterton too
just down the track where wanders the fools
the Barnes built the houses and the village was famed
with its tales of the back woods and the fairground that came
but the farm has its place in the halls of the famed

Ray Wills

Within her lovers arms

Her dress it was of scarlet red
and her eyes were so sea blue
she lived upon the heather lands
not far from the old Sea View

Her sisters were of the meadow lands
and her brothers were raised upon the fells
her voice was like the birds at dawn
and her heart was so forlorn

She loved him like no other then
he took her breath away
she lost him to her heart and soul
and then he rode away

Shed met him on the Ferris wheel
for fairgrounds were their life
the swish backs and the bumper cars
the swing boats and the rides
the galleries with their little ducks
the stars that lit the skies

She lost him to the pretty girls
and the fortune telling kind
he took her in his arms that day
he promised her the world
he was the loving kind

then he loved her in the deepest woods
was then he rode away
She wore the look of love that day
she wore the look of pain
the sky was dark and fearsome
and the clouds were full of rain

The crows were in their nests that night
she took herself to mourning then
put away her bright red dress
she lost her soul and lover then
within the Gypsy's arms
he rode away to freedom then
with all his Gypsy charms

Ray Wills

I left the deafening noise of the fair well behind me and entered the woodland there were no lights on in the cottage. Had i left it too late i wondered and had Mary gone to bed. As i got close to the cottage i saw there was actually a small light on in the front porch. I stood at the door and gently lifted the heavy knocker and tapped it hard on the door. All was silent. I was just about to turn and go look for an Inn to stay for the night when i heard a soft voice behind me. "Ow he be then me darlin" "did you have a nice time at the fair." It was the distinctive voice of Mary. She was standing close behind me and I noticed that she was shorter than me and was wearing a darker dress now. She touched my hand and spoke "Come follow me ere, i be got your bicycle in the back ere"she said, "but spec yould like a hot chocolate"," il put it on the hearth for you,"she said. "Come follow me."

Then she led me to the side of the cottage down a side lane which itself led to a small latch door. She lifted the latch and opened the door and ushered me inside. As i entered the room i noticed the small fancy kerosene welcoming lamp which lit up the small room. It was warm inside and then i saw there was a fireplace with flaming logs. It was a nicely decorated room with draped red curtains an old fashioned sofa and the two armchairs with fancy red embroadered cushions. "Make yourself comfy love" she said "Il just go get us a drink."

As she left the room i notied she went into another small door I sat back into the soft well cushioned sofa and realised just how i needed to relax.

She returned to the room sometime later with a wooden tray with two hot steaming tankard cups. She looked quite different now. She now had on a white light cotton blouse which showed off her shapely figure well. And a blue thin skirt which although ankle length had a split at the side which when she moved showed off her shapely long legs. She was barefoot. She brought one of the hot tankard drinks from the tray to me and put it into my hand. "There you be and here i be"she said as she sat on the edge of the sofa next to me."Thanks" i said and sipped the hot chocolate. "Its very nice" i said. "It should be" she said," i do put a little cream and honey syrup in it specly ". "Your bicycles is in the cupboard agaInt the wall" she said." "Ok thanks" i said.

"You been Bere afore aint you" she said "Yes i have "i answered.

"It be quiet here" she said "except for the fair days, like now." I nodded my head in agreement.

She sat drinking her chocolate smiling at me as she did so. With her blue eyes and fair hair she looked very attractive in the firelight glow. I thought back to earlier in the Iday. To the moment when she walked away from me recalling how the light from the sun had shone directly upon her thin cotton dress showed up her partly naked body under her dress.

I couldn't help but notice that now she was looking at me deeply. Staring into my eyes with a puzzled expression on her face as though she was trying to suss me out.

"Your strange but nice" she said. " Am i " i answered.

"Yes, she said, "but dun know why you be wearing those foreign clothes," "You bant be French be you."

" No" i replied. "I'm English." Mary spoke"You be gypsy bant you," she asked. "Yes i am" i answered. "There be lots of gypsy up ere today" she said "My family comes down from them Fancey peoples," "they be gypsy" she said. I nodded.

She touched my hand gently and her light blue eyes looked directly into mine. Then she asked me "Would you be minding very much, if I do ask ya summit personal." "No" i said, "though it depends what it is."

"Well" she said "You baint said nu thin bout the fair and where else you been" "n if you had nice time or not" "Or even told me your name," "you does have a name,don't you" she asked, giving me a cheeky smile at the same time."Oh yes of course" i replied, "its Raymond."

"That be nice name " she replied "sounds posh."

I replied "Thanks" "and yes" I said " It was great at the fair."

Then i told her all about Thomas Hardy's visit and about the man who swore at me over by the gypsy site.

She replied, "Oh that be olé Ged Bartlett." "His people do run the fair, he be gypsy too" "He do employs the fairground show gypsies n he was morn likely seeing after them you."

"Oh", i answered," I think they are from the Gallows hill site down Bere road." "I know lots Travelling Gypsies used the

encampment on Gallows hill encampment" I said and then said the familiar names I knew of. The Skemps,Stanley's,Penfolds, Burton's,Burdens,Issacs,Mayne,Fletcher,Boswell's,Roberts,Hughes and Franklin's. She seemed to be surprised at my knowledge. Then I told her. " I had passed the camp earlier, Mary." She smiled and said, "Yes that be right they do live there." "you know a lot them".I answered her. "I know of some of them."
She said," It was once a very bad place." "What do you mean Mary " I asked," how bad." "She said. "Well there was once a Judge hereabouts name of Jefferies,he who hung folks up there on the gallows"she said. "They did call him the hanging judge, " "I do think he lived and worked in Dorchester at the assizes," "least that's what folks do say." "Yes your right" I said. She asked me."You baint married be you"?

She was now looking deeply into my eyes. "No I'm not married Mary, no one well have me" I said and smiled."You do got nice eyes and i love your dimple," she said. Then she asked me. "You ain't jump sticks then"? she giggled, "No i haven't" i said. "Do you have a boyfriend Mary "i asked." She answered me "Why, no", "What ya mean, do i have a lover?" "I not been anyone,there be no nice boys in village, they be all dinlos n nappos."she said. I smiled and she held my hand."I once had me a fine young man" she said, " His name were John Torville, he were me lover, my husband like " "But he fought a ways in wars and never came home." "We had two boys." "I lost one at birth he was called William and the other Tom he died of the bad illness that were in village few years back." "He was just three then when he died very small "she sad"

Oh I'm sorry Mary " I replied."That be alright she said , I am over it now, was long time past." She looked directly at me then asked "You tell fortunes" "No",its women folks job to do them." I replied.

"That be Pity" she said and moved closer towards me on the sofa. I smiled at her. Then she slid her body on the sofa so she was much closer to me. I could smell the aroma sweetness of her floral lavender scent. It was unlike any that i had smelt before. As I held her hand and looked into her eyes she lent slightly forward. As she did so I could see within her open top blouse. She was completely naked there and I saw her lovely breasts. Then I realised that she had been sat here with her top naked all the time. Then as she lent closer towards me, our bodies met and our lips locked in a passionate kiss. I undid her few remaining dress buttons with my fingers as we kissed and I caressed her breasts with my hands. She sighed with pleasure and I felt her hands gripping my shoulders tightly. Then with her hand holding mine she hastily led me across the room then into her little bedroom.

Marys bedroom was furnished with soft blue lavender pillows and colourful rugs. Her bed was a large brass four poster iron framed. The bedclothes were of light cotton decorated and embroadered with pretty light blue lace. The mattress and eiderdown were both of duck feather down.

Then she was there on the bed besides me. Spreading out her naked body before me. She smiled at me invitingly and said "Take me, I be all yours my gypsy lover " I be all yours."

So it was that my time travels had taken me to the worst of places and tonight it was to the best of places. As i lay with the lovely Mary Fancey.

I awoke in the featherdown bed,in the early hours, naked and refreshed. I turned over and as i did so. I once again saw her naked body stretched out next to me. Her eyes half open and dreamy. She smiled at me then she reached out to me and she cuddled her body into mine. Then we both fell back into a deep sleep.

Then when i awoke next it was morning. I was woken up by the sun shining its rays into the bedroom window and the sound of a cockbirds crowing in the farm below. I looked for her, but she was gone, nowhers to be seen. Along with the taste of and the womanly scent of Mary Fancey.

I made my way out to the yard and found the scullery with its deep stone sink and washed myself with the cold water and the large block of green soap. Soap which also had the distinct smell of carbolic along with a hint of lavender. Then back in the bedroom I hurriedy dressed and as i did so i heard the familiar sound in the distance of the church bells. I thought of the service in the high church its ceremonial customs of members of its hooded choir. Along with its prayer mats for knelling on and its incense. Not forgetting the services of hell and damnation for all sinners. It was a thrill i didnt want to experience again. I went to the large cupboard and took out my raleigh bike. I noticed that it was well cared for. For Mary had even cleaned off all the mud from its tyres. I made the bed as best i could and then made my way out through the door and into the front outside amongst the tall trees. All was quiet except for the wood pidgeons in the distance and some chickens pecking and roosting nearby.I mounted my bike, checked its gears and slowly began the decent of the long winding steep hill down the long track into the village. When i reached the village i saw the Revd Montague Ackland Bere with his young wife and their small children. All making their way from the vicarage at the rear of west street. Where in the long distant future would stand the hall and apartments of Cyril wood court.They were joined by many villages also making their way to the church. All the men dressed in black suits and the women with thir faces shielded by fine linen drapes each one also clutching a black bible. Then they crossed the road and went down the little stoney lane past the stables and towards the church. They were all dressed neatly in their sunday best. All very formal and each held tighty their own large black bible. I called out "Good morning" and they called back "Good morning." With Revd Bere adding " Young man" "Are you attending todays service." I never replied and rode on up to Rye hill passing by the Bere stream on the way with its little stone and wooden bridge. On my left was the farm in the distance with its large white thatched farmhouse its cow shed and dairy. It was deserted now no sign of life and its meadows very still. For the cows had no doubt all slowly sauntered and drifted along wafting their tails at the flys as they all made their ways to be milked.As cows do. There they all no doubt gathered themselves into the cow shed and dairy. Where the lovely Mary Fancey was no doubt to be very busy. Along with the other young dairy maids hand milking the cows. An act which they did regularly seven days a week.

    Soon i had changed my gears on the bike and was heading to the top of the steep hill passing the deserted village school on my left. On reaching the top of the hill i stopped at the entrance to the Rye farm. Where i knew in many later years a friend Kevin

Crocker and his lady wife Amanda would live.Managing the farm and its busy restaurant and shop.

Then i noticed the large board sign outside the main gate of the entrance. I stopped riding my bike and looked at the sign. It was very old and consisted of a detailed list of various vermin and their prices. Obviously many poor villagers along with gypsies depended on these ways to make a living.

The sign read

RYE FARM
proprieter Samuel House
Vermins extertmination prices.

"To all local villagers of Bere.
Bring your vermin heads here wanted for good money.
We pay for sparrows, rats, beavers, moles, foxes, badgers, polecats, weasils.
Heads, two pennies each, 30 pennies for ten vermins."

The list went on and on. It was signed at the very bottom by an official dignatory. Which consisted of a scrawled handwritten signature of a Mr A Bartlett village clerk. Then an official stamp of the squire by the name of Drax he being the landlord of Bere. I noticed that it had the crest coat of arms at the top of the sign with its familiar standing lion with crown and with name within it of Dur be ville. The date stamp was very old 1786.

Thereafter i made the decision to take a circular route. For I wanted to see once again the famous Drax wall of the Lord Drax one reknowned in these parts as being the wealthy lord of the manor.

I got back on my bike and took a turning to the left. After cycling for sometime through narrow hedgegrow lanes. I found myself cycling on a very long stretch of a road. To my left views of meadows and to my right was a long and high brick wall which seemed to go on forever. I knew from my own readings that this was built by French prisoners of war in the Napoleonic war. Then i reached the end of the wall the familiar high stone entrance pillars of the Drax estate. With its majestic distinctive five legged antlered stag deer proudly displayed on the top of its pillars. This was the boundary wall estate of the famed wealthy landlord Drax .Where rumour had it that the lord Drax could only see three legs of the deer from his manor house. This didnt please him and it was said that he had them craft an extra leg. So he could view the normal four legs of the stag. It was said that he had made his great wealth by means of the slave trade. Along with his many foreign plantations in far away places such as the Drax hall estate Barbados. This sugar plantation has been in the Drax family for over 3 centuries. During which time the owners imposed countless cruelties on enslaved Africans and their descendants.

One of the modern day historians said that "The Drax family has done more harm and violence to the black people of Barbados than any other family. The Draxes built and designed and structured slavery."

After studying the wall and the entrance pillars for a while I got back on my bike and continued the journey. I wondered if the hard dark red bricks of the wall were all built by the slave labour of local gypsy brick makers and laborers sweat. I wondered how many brickyards did Drax and the other landowners have in those days. And how many poor young men worked these pits and mannings to meet his requirements for this 3 mile wall. The number of bricks used on the wall surrounding the Drax estate must have been gone into three million or more. These poor souls no doubt worked for years to create these bricks for his wall. I was aware that there were three brickyards in Bere alone but there were many more in the area and these bricks were all of local dark red clay. All those bricks wasted on a wall when they could have been used to house hundreds of folk. Reminds me of one of these modern day popularist politicans whose chant was "build that wall".

I cycled on the country lanes passing through small villages all with just a few thatched roofed dwellings a church and a number of farms.The meadows were plentiful and the hedgegrows were full of bird song.

My thoughts were of Mary Fancey and wondered if i would ever see her again in my travels. I felt that i had left her without any explanation. But i knew it would be impossible to stay with her at Bere or to try and explain to her what i was experiencing. For i knew that very soon i would once again travel off in the vardo dream wagon into another place in time.

   I wondered if Mary Fancey was an ancestor of long ago a relative of my great great grandfather Gideon Fancy.

CHAPTER FIVE

CHILDHOOD DAYS

Childhood Days

Charlie Eaton brought the pig swill
from the finest hotels in the land
Sankey Moody chopped the finest meat
at his butcher home by hand
delivered to your door

Mary Mabey made the finest floral wreaths
and splendid fine displays
to celebrate your new romance
and your lovely wedding day

We all shopped at up on hill
Us kids all attended the Regal cinemas
matinees each Saturday
Rogers was the warden at the St Clements church
he ushered folks out before the service ended
he drove them all a ways

The fairground was at the Branksome rec every holiday
it was where we spent our pennies
and passed our youth away
constitution was our sea view
we could look through the periscope each and ever day
view Poole harbour and the Purbeck hills
many miles away

Bill Knott made the caravans
and we took them on the roads

Ryvita crispbread factory just across the lane
where the Gypsy Queen Caroline Hughes parked
with the Warrens, the Turners and Kings heavy wagon loads

Ray Wills

Gypsy Childhood

My aunt Mary Mabey made the flower wreaths
and the flowers for the shows
Aunt Macey Castle read the tea leaves then
it seems so long ago

Uncle Bill Rogers he told the stories and yarns all fit for a king
My granfer Reg made the bricks back then
My great Aunt King was a Gypsy Queen

My great grandmother Emily was a Lady
she wore her Fancy clothes
they made a roads name after her
it was so long ago

My long time grandfather Jim Hansford
he was a tall strong man
he lived upon the moors
worked with his hands

My cousin Jean was a dancer
she was the Queen of Poole carnival show
her brother George a school chorister
and school organ maker too
my uncle Sid rode in the Monte Carlo Rally
he acted crazy
but he was nobody's fool
My aunt Vera was a Dominey
she lived in one of grandfather houses
he had many from Newtown to Alderney

Great uncle Harry was a house builder by trade
my father was a romantic he wrote letters
and a champion played the darts
he was a fine tree surgeon
nearly fell to his grave

Our landlord was old Cedric Hughes
his mother was a gypsy Queen
whilst the artist John Augustus
at Alderney Manor
painted our house known as heather view
before we all lived on the Mannings Heath
with such a lovely view of Poole

Ray Wills

Cousins

My cousins they were gypsies
we played upon the heaths
where the grass it grew so tall
the heathers were so sweet

The elder was a lady
a queen of Poole grand show
they paid her tributes daily
everywhere she go-ed

She danced at Zena Martel's
she had a voice so rare
she talked n talked for hours
spent evenings at the fair

She learned to twist the paper
make flowers oh so rare
floral bouquets for your wife
flowers for her hair

Her brother sang on television
they made it on the show
built the organ at Kemp Welch
choir boy on the radio

Their father was a Gypsy
their mother was a maid
their grandma was the Gypsy queen
flowers on her grave

Ray Wills

Bye gone Artist

They called me the artist as a kid
classroom chatter broken nibs
teachers rhetoric maths and fun
stand up for the Queen be a man my son

They called me an artist with the eye
swift and neat pencilled skies
Disney characters playground fun
skipping games country runs

Cricket, soccer, catch that ball
teachers pet and prayers in the hall
detention for talking
go stand outside the masters door

They called me the artist as a kid
naked ladies were the best i did
my pictures floated around the class
now I am in trouble what a blast

They called me the artist as a kid
I sketched the church and river Frome
kissed the girls then walked them home
i drew the teachers rude and free
bare boobs and lots of revelry

They called me the artist as a kid
great imagination and perfect lines
popular and fun in perfect time
don't daydream boy get in line

Ray Wills

I awoke from my sleep in the vardo wagon. This time to find myself once again a small kid living on the Mannings heath. Here I was happy spending many hours accompanied by my Airedale dogs. Taking them out rabbiting with my ferrets(which I carried in a pouch in my deep trouser pockets). Often on such excursions with my uncles Bill and Tony Rogers and the Gypsies the Turners and Warrens. Who were young men and close relatives of the Gypsy songsters Caroline Hughes. These were friends of our family and I went with them regularly rabbiting over the common up at lodge hills. On those excursions we took nets and of course I brought my ferrets. Many of these Gypsy families were roaming the area with their Vardos wagon's, horses and dog pack's. There were Gypsy site's scattered throughout the terrain from Newtown up to to Canford Magna where Lady Wimborne had her Manor. I spent much time amongst them all and watched as they caught hedgehogs which they called hotchi. Taking them from out amongst the dead leaves or dry grasses in the bushes. Then they killed them by uncurling them and smashing their nose with a stick. Then their sharp prickles they burnt off before they were covered with wet clay. Before being placed in the hot ashes of the yog fire then cooked. I loved eating them, they tasted like pork and chicken.

I watched as gypsy travellers created their bender homes. They chose the best of the young hazel. Some of these benders were so high you could stand in them. The doors was of sacking and they sometimes used old army blankets as coverings as they were waterproof or else tarpaulin. These benders were always very warm and comfortable inside.

I lived with my brought up by my grandparents Reg and Alice Roger. Along with their sons Bill and Tony and their daughter Bessie. The elder brother Billy was known as the storyteller. He was also skilled in the building of bird houses bird nesting boxes and aviary's. He had hordes of nest boxes full of young canaries, gold finches and miners. Folks came to him from miles away to buy these young birds who sang beautifully. Bill could put his hand to most things practical as well as being a fine darts and card player. He also liked a flutter on the gee gees too and was often in the bookies. Uncles Bill Rogers Prize pigeons were taken on our excursions to Exeter in large cane basket when we visited our relations there (the Thorpe's) each year. Then we would set these free from the basket as we left Exeter. With them arriving back at the Mannings pigeon and dove lofts well before our arrival home. Bill was also known to be a bit of a scrapper and got into many a fight. He worked the brick yards clay pits and iron foundries locally. As well as being a very good lorry driver for his cousin Sid at Rogers transport. Bill passed away a day before his 90th birthday he smoked woodbines for most of his life. Bill was renowned for his tales. He could spin a yarn or rhyme that seemed to never end.

These are a few I remember.

Once upon a time

Once upon a time when the bees drank wine
when the monkeys chewed tobacco
a little birdie came with a feather up his bum
to see what was the matter

ANON

Three old crows

Three old crows sat on a tree
as black as crows could very well be
they all flew over a desert plain
they landed on a donkeys lane
they all alighted on his backbone
they pecked his eyes out one by one
out came the farmer with his gun
he shot those crows excepting one
that old crow he flew away
il tell you the rest some other day

ANON

Outside a Lunatic Asylum

Outside a lunatic asylum
I had a job braking up stones
along comes a lunatic
and says to me how are you Mr Jones
how much a week do you get for doing this
thirty bob a week I cried
thirty bob a week half a dozen kids to keep
come inside you silly fellow come inside

ANON

Uncle Tony Rogers, Bills younger brother hardly attended school spending his childhood on the heath with his dogs. I remember this story about him when I was a kid.

"Well that's that sorted Alice" said grandad to his wife Alice."What Reg"she said. "I've taken that boy to school Alice" he said. "What do you mean Reg, he's been here for ages"she replied. "What do you mean woman" he said "I took the car and I drove him to school and took him in the gates and I just came back by car". Alice answered him "Well whose that out there on the common with the dogs then look out of the window Reg". Reg got up from his chair and he gazed out the living room window. Yes she was right he thought. There he was over on the common chasing with the dogs. Then he said "Well I never woman". "What are we going to do with him seems he don't like school just like all the other gypsy kids".

Uncle Tony once drew me aside and told me. "Our Dads people the Rogers originally came to Kinson from the New Forest" "They went through hard times there and had moved to Kinson to make a new life for themselves."

Even then Tony had the gift of prophecy as he told me. " In years to come all this Canford heath land will all be built on, there will be be nothing but houses" "There will be cinemas close by and big shops."

I never took him serious then but he was so right. For years later the area became known as Tower Park with cinemas and shopping malls. He also told me "In years to come when your old" "Long after my time the Chinese will be the richest country in the world with great armies and rulers."

I regularly visited Uncle Sid Rogers at his local transport companies' lorry yard (Rogers Transport) in fancy road. (the road named after my great grandmother Emily Fancy).Then afterwards I dropped in on Uncle Charlie Rogers at his large pigsties nearby at Wool Road. The Rogers families operated numerous brick yards and builders enterprises over the years. We were all closely related to George, Harry, Lester, John and Sid. As well as many other local travelling families.

Gran told me "The brickyards had all originated from your great grandmothers Emily Fancy Rogers first pig and the growth of the original smallholding farm". "Culminating in the family brickyard on the Manning s Heath". "Where our Mannings home is with its few few acres of small holding farm". The brickyards tall chimney was a focal point in the local landscape and could be seen from the trains carriage windows passing trough at Poole railway station.

There was so many animals at the Mannings there were dogs, cats, rabbits, ferrets, ducks, chickens, geese, bird aviaries and a loft. With canaries,doves and pigeons, cows, pigs, ponies and goats.

I collected chickens eggs, hot from under the wings of hens as well as feeding and scattering their corn ,often mucking out of the pigs in their sties. The laying down of fresh hay in the cow shed as bedding. Along with the mixing of meal and pigs swill (which grandad bought monthly from Charlie Eaton from the large Bournemouth hotels). Then dropping it into the deep copper of boiling water in the copper house. All cooked in the boiling hot copper house oven, ready for the pigs' dinners. I loved the rich sweet smell of this concoction.

I assisted with the wheel borrowing of pig manure, to fill in the trenches at the smallholdings allotment gardens. The planting of seeds, gardening work, or the collection of fruit, from the trees in the two vast orchards. I assisted Grandfather with the brick building of the front garden wall. And with my uncles on the the new pig sties and often with the construction of new hen pens, ready for the housing of hundreds of chickens.

Grandad never allowed any of our dogs in the house just like most travellers they kept to these old ways. Bad language was never allowed in the Manning household. Grandad said "Such gutter language should stay out in the gutter where it belonged". He was quick to condemn the modern space travellers. "Things high up in the sky had no right being there". He said "It would lead to pollution and change nature". Like nuclear testing he said that "It was against God". Injections were also frowned upon. As was constant bathing or showering as grandad said it weakened the body". The chemical use like DDT and powdered fertilisers much used by farmers at the time he condemned. He said "it killed the soil"." It wasn't natural" he said and he was adamant "that the best fertiliser was animal dung". He moved the chicken pens regularly to avoid any diseases and made sure the water troughs were always full of clean water for the hens. He was opposed to scientists creating and testing diseases he said that "at some time in the future they would create a disease" "and it would escape"." Millions would die from it". He had been an active member of the non conformist Christians when a young man. As well as joining secret society's. He also was a good darts player attending many tournaments with my father William Hansford .Who was the son of the strongman Jim Hansford.

Grandfather bought himself a new pony and had staked it out close by our house under an electrical pylon. Then in the morning when he awoke and had dressed and was on his way downstairs for breakfast. He looked out of the landing window at the pony in the distance. He was concerned that there was something moving around close to the pony. He hurried out and crossed to where the pony was tethered and as he drew closer he saw that it was a new born pony. For unbeknown to him the pony had given birth overnight. Now he had a bargain two ponies for the price of one.

Granfer told the oldest folklore tales ever. Such as " The cuckoos that comes in the spring lives in the meadows of Stoborough in Wareham and it isn't until the farmer opens the gates there and lets them all out that we see and hear the cuckoos".

All the grand kids would sit on granfers lap and on the floor and he would tell them all such tall stories. He called this place his coopy house. Granfer was constantly warning me "Ray be careful on the heath boy, there's a store of hidden ammunition, abandoned on the boggy heath" "Left over from the war years, grenades and mines embedded in the heathland mossy blanket;be careful".

Many of my my young school mates were collecting birds eggs from the commons and blowing them out. leaving just a shell. Building up fine collections they proudly showed off to everyone. "You must not do that" my grandfather had told me. "Your school mates are in fact stealing and killing and destroying young birds by this act". "It is against nature and an offence".

Gran kept a rich source of herbs and natural medicines for all manner of ailments in a small pantry under the stairs. Including bottles of herbal medicines, jars of nettle tea, blackcurrant juice, camphor oil and cabbage water to ward off winter colds. Along with candles and large tins of black molasses treacle. "How old are you Gran" I once asked. She replied, as always, " I'm as that way old as my tongue and a little older than my teeth" she would always reply that way. "What's for tea Gran" I asked. To which she would often reply, "Rounders around the table and back again."

I helped Gran with the making of Christmas puddings, cooked in the deep stone kitchen copper, using sheeting's of cotton to tie them up, before being cooked in large saucepans and the copper itself.

On autumn months with Gran I dragged my home made wooden boxed go-karts .and sacks up high to the lodge hill banks. To collect sacks of fallen fir cones from the heathers. There were multitudes there, of all shapes and sizes and all dried out from the sun. They made excellent fire starters for the cold winter months at the Mannings. Then I would drag these heavy-laden carts, down the winding sandy tracks of heather to the Mannings house coal shed, for winter storage as firewood.

I was able to to roam miles in complete safety and our Mannings house front door often remained unlocked at night. Grandad would be more concerned with the foxes, which occasionally came to the Mannings during the early Hershey would drag off chickens to their lairs high up in the banks of lodge hills at Canford Magna.

I was regularly involved with groups of kids on the heath many of whom were gypsies. In the building of underground dens in the sandy mounds. Such as at the rear of the local Trent companies car dump at the rear of the man ringwood road. Charlie Trent's displayed a large placard billboard out on the main Ringwood road declaring it to be the largest in Europe. Our underground dens were all padded out on the inside, with mattresses and carpets. They were covered on top with a galvanise tin sheeting this covered by sods of grass as camouflage. Trees we conquered and used for rope Tarzan swings. From their high branches hung ropes with abandoned car tyres, or a stick as the seat. It rotated in large circular movements with a high drop below with safe sandy surfaces below. Another favourite play place of us kids was the rear of the nearby Alderney Hospital grounds here there was was a large abandoned red sandy quarry area. The sweet smelling scent of the pines was seen as a cure for tuberculosis and many sanatoriums were built locally such as at Alderney Hospital. This play site was actually a reservoir which we often used for playing games and adventurous pursuits. Building camps and dens and caves into the sides of its quarry's sandy red banks. Often we all swam naked here with little care or modesty completely innocent in this safe pool of water. Such places were our adventure playgrounds then.

   At weekends and holidays myself and cousins the Domineys, went cockling in the backwaters of Poole at Hamworthy. It was a muddy occupation, but so enjoyable for me as small kid. It involved the search for cockles, amongst the muddy seashore, gathering them into tin buckets and sacks.

   I wore Wellington boots as a nipper and with members of the family walked along the Ringwood road to Wimborne market escorting a herd of our cows to sell there. Through Bere cross, Longham and Ferndown. With my large stick and wearing my wellington boots. Another time we went across the heath to the expanse of open water, known as Waterloo. To buy a pig the ugly giant boar with big teeth which we called' Waterloo George'. Another time we went there and brought home a new nanny goat with collar and long metal chain. Which grandad had bought from one of his lady friends there. We had caught a double-decker bus on the old Wareham road with our three dogs and the goat. We all clambered up to the top floor of the bus much to the amusement of the passengers and the bus conductor. An event that one could not so easily do in our present society.

There were hidden dangers also, included the quick sand clay. When my young toddler sister visited, and I took her for a stroll across an abandoned clay pit, at the rear of the family brickyard. She was strong willed I told her "Your not to go there". But she ignored me and soon found that she had trapped herself in an area of quicksand. I tried to reach her, but found myself slipping in, fortunately I had called for help. Then the local brickyards watchman, appeared with a strong length of rope and fortunately managed to haul her free. We went home with our skins baked in red clay and quick sand. My sister was lifted and scrubbed by my mother in the deep stone kitchen sink.

One hot summers day I found a box of matches and caught fire to some furze bushes on the common, which terrified me. I was unable to put the fire out, it was spreading so fast before my eyes, eventually three fire engines arrived. I was kept in my room and scolded for this major misdemeanour. And I was determined in later years to provide safe play opportunities for children, to both control fires and to enjoy the excitement, energy and warmth of fires within supervised adventure playground environments.

The local schools at Branksome heath and Kemp Welch in the Rossmore area have a high number of kids from gypsy travelling families. Many of whom would bunk off school regularly. Preferring to chase their pack of dogs and go off rabbiting on the heaths than sit in a classroom.

At Branksome heath school I was known by my classmates as the artist. Having a special aptitude for drawing and copying any picture to perfection. I would swiftly sketch some of the young student lady teachers. Always skilfully drawing them in nude sketches and always with more than their share of ample boobs. These drawings went the round of my classroom mates both boys and girls to their delight. Until one day the teacher caught one my class mates with one of these in his hand. Once the teacher saw it he knew straight a ways it was of my handy work. I was kept in after the school was finished for the day. Arriving late at my Mannings home. Unbeknown to me one of the teachers lived as close neighbour to my uncles lady friend and had told her. So that when I got home I was chastised and sent to my room.

I was just a kid on the heath with my dogs,and my ferrets. Just an artist with my uncanny gift of being able to create drawings. These were of politicians, Disney's cartoon characters, daily mirrors Andy Capp or pretty sexy ladies. I would draw to perfection with my tongue sticking out to help my concentration. All our relatives when visiting would ask to see my art creations.

Travellers and show people the Kings, Castles and Mabeys were relatives. They lived for a time close by one another in a neat row of cottages called "The terrace" situated on the Ringwood road at Newtown. Before they moved to live at Arne avenue and in later years on the Trinidad estate. Mary Mabey uncle Georges Castles sister became well known locally for making exquisite floral wreaths and wedding bouquets for the local community and was well respected in the area.

Uncle Georges Castles mother Annabella was known as Bella . She was said to have been extremely attractive when young. But was very dark and foreboding in old age and scary to me now as a small boy. Each time she visited I was scared of her and hid under the front room table. I heard grandad calling my name as he walked with her looking for me. She loved kids although her language was very course. Granfer eventually found me and said "Come on Raymond your Aunt wants to see you" . I crept out from the table scared. She saw me and smiled, her face was very very dark and lined. Then she spoke in a strange way you said "Here you are my Raymond."In her hand she held out a large silver coin. She said " Here's a present for you" I took the coin from her dark scrawny hand. "Thank you" I said. She then said "don't I get a kiss then my Raymond". She bent down to my level and I reluctantly kissed her face and ran back under the safety of the table. Till the next time.

I often visited the Castles at Arne Avenue. Which at night is somewhere where a small boy shouldn't frequent. On this one time I was just leaving their Arne avenue home one dark evening. The street lights there were quiet unusual for they gave out an eerie shade of light. I had not gone far on my route back to Alderney. When I heard children's voices and then found myself approached by a small group of children older than myself. None of whom I recognised. Obviously the streets in this area were very territorial. They approached me with the taller of the boys pointing his index finger into my face and spoke. "What you doing here mush you ain't from here are you". "No "I replied" I am going home". They all laughed and gathered around me there were five of them, three boys and two girls. "Piss off then" the smaller boy said,he was around my age probably seven or eight years old. The taller boy then asked me "What's your name mush" he came closer and pushed me hard with his hand, a smart smack on my shoulder. "I'm Ray" I said. They all laughed and formed a closed circle around me. Then one of the girls spoke "Give him a good smacking Brian"," he's not from our way" he's not one us". The other smaller of the two girls spoke,"No you shouldn't be here, your not one of us mush, you be a diddy koy". Than they all laughed "yeh a dirty thieving kier". I was scared, for they were now all poking me with their fingers. I felt fear, being cornered by this gang of kids with no one around to help. So I panicked and clenching my right hand into a fist i swung a punch at the elder taller boy who stood the closest to me. As a result of which I felt the flesh of his nose as my fist smacked into it with some force. Then the dark red blood shot out from his nose and as it did he bent forward and cried. The girls called me all manner of terrible names, many I had never heard the likes of before. I hurriedly darted out of the group whilst they were more concerned with the state of their injured friend. And I ran off down the road as fast as my legs could take me, up the avenue towards the main Herbert avenue. I never once looked back. Then very soon I found myself on the avenue and felt safe. I was still shaking from the experience as I made my way onto the busy Ringwood road. After crossing the road I headed down towards the familiar safety of the gorse bush lined track of the Manning s heath road. Then to the safety of our home the Mannings there in the yard sat the little vardo dream wagon.

CHAPTER SIX

UPON THE DOWNS

Royal Blood Roma

They say she had royal blood running in her veins
she was born on the heath one Saturday
they say she was true Romani bred
she picked the flowers
she made the wreaths and beds

She lived in a vardo amongst gaily painted wooden van and sheds
fancy lamps and brassy urns tall stories in the morn
they said she was rich in dreams and fortune telling games
she planted herbs and knew all their fancy Latin names

They do say she grew up rich in tales and fancy rhymes
sing us a song Roma tell us a rhyme

They said her parents were of the Dominey and Sherwood breed
teachers of the pulpit flowers in the sheds
her brothers and her sisters worked the farmers lands
hops and fruit I will tell you your fortune give me your hands
the heaths were rich and the fields were free
stopping places Atchen Tans such a history
then write it down for all to see

Ray Wills

The Gypsy Girl

She was the Gypsy girl with common tongue
dialect sweet and full of fun
played on the heaths where rabbits run
where fox were chased by masters race
it was said for sport and was disgraced

The Gypsy girl was up fore dawn
when sun and dew blessed each morn
where chaffinch thrush sand in the broom
where bees did buzz and crickets sang
their songs of love to mortal man

The Gypsy girl was born to dance
castanets and accordions played their true romance
where vardos decked the feathered floors
of commons rich to local lords

The Gypsy girl dark with beauty eyes
sang her songs to gnats and flies
amongst the bracken birch and briers
whilst gathering sticks for the yog and fire

Where blackberries rich were hanging free
upon the downs like Rosemary
the Gypsy girl was rich in love
her dreams were strong and her dance was free
upon the land where God set thee

Ray Wills

I woke up from a deep sleep and stepped outside of the vardo wagon.

Now i found myself in very unfamiliar surroundings for i was at the Epsom races. An event which is known as 'The greatest flat race in the world'. I had never been to a race meeting before. Up to some 130,000 people could attend here. Which Charles Dickens was said to have once attended. The trial of the greatest horse Eclipse once took place here too. It was so early that no one saw it apart from an old Gypsy woman. She told the racing touts that no other contestants could catch up with him even if they ran to the worlds end. There is a local traditon that the name of the Derby winner is chalked on the wall of the local pub on the morning prior to the race. It is believed to be a Gypsy tradition dating back many decades.

There were hundreds of lower class or working class folks here today. All sporting their familiar cloth caps, jackets and breachs trousers with high laced shoes. All of them jostling and gathering in family groups so noisy and exciteable. Most them having saved their hard earned monies to attend this great occassion. And no doubt to wager their cash on some nag last at the post. What surprised me most was the noise of the crowds and the crowds were so big, the very green expanse of grass. The horses here were so much taller than the cobs and the ponies in the gypsy sites i knew in my childhood. Considering the vast crowds here, it is surprising there is so little crime. Though race gangs have slashed and brawled, bookmakers have run away to welsh on their customers and been beaten up when caught. Whilst pickpockets preferred to do their work right under the eyes of the less observant constables.

Hundreds of folks had put on their finest fashions today as usual to watch the thoroughbred colts and fillies race the mile-long track.

Then I saw the authorised Gypsy site set up to the west of the Grandstand.

It was one of the largest concentrations of Gypsies I had ever seen. There must be a few hundred here today I thought. I chatted with a gypsy who told me that he had seen as many as 1,500 people here. Those here today wre living in mainly very basic wagons and carts with tarpaulin roofing. Gypsies always were regular visitors here and a major public attraction over the years. With their family gatherings, horse trading deals and flower selling. Not to mention all heir boots with the fortune telling attractions. They were obviously a very popular added attraction for the general public. Also with their amazing sometimes accurate racing tips,entertainment along with their lucky charms. I was surprised to see so many gypsy flower girls here today with their large baskets full of the finest of flowers.I recognised the familiar families characteristics of the Whites, Coles, Kings, Boswells, Croutchers and Coles amongst them. Though often gypsies were seen as rogues or lawbreakers yet here tis discrimisation seemed to be absent at these Derby races.

Up on the higher ground was the fairground with all its usual attractions.

With fortune-telling still being carried on there no doubt by the granddaughters or great-grand-daughters of the famous Rose Lee or Petulengro.The booth where the fortune-teller Old Kate was often visited by Royalty and received soverigns for her predictions. For many years royalty have maintained this royal tradition of tipping of a sovereign to the gypsies. And now there were placard boards which advertised the greatest of these queens as being that of the fortune tellers of royalty. I saw the familiar Gypsy woman with the flashing red or yellow handkerchief on her head and the strange silvery hoarse voice worked the crowd now. She was carrying a baby with her whilst her other children minded her tent. I got talking to some gypsies nearby who told me that their families here today included amongst them the Boswells,Lees,Marleys,Jessops,Davises,Penfolds and Gilberts.

I knew that Gypsy families were renowned in these fairgrounds enterprises like the swingboats they managed. These being the Cole's,Bartlett's, Kings, Castles, James and Hills. All were all busy working these family enterprises today. A gypsy nearby told me that the Prince of Wales and future king/Edward had once attended the races and his horse won. And that on that particular day, many of the Gypsy woman danced for him. Including Granny Waters and her two sisters from the new forest. They danced beneath the grandstand where he had his party. Shaking tambourines, and they were all dressed 'all colours of the rainbow'. They danced beneath a shower of coins, including many sovereigns flung down to them by the royal party. Granny Walters and her sisters would take fifty pounds a day dancing at these race meetings. She would dance inspired then by guitar playing and singing of Green Broom, a song always close to the Romanies heart. The gypsy woman told me Granny Walters wore a rusty black hat with curls of wiry grey hair pressing beneath it. With big pins ornamenting the crown, brass ear-rings glinting amongst her hair, an old riding habit type of coat and long skirts. She would lift up her skirts as she danced an old step-dance, she showed the legs which delighted a king. Another gypsy woman present told me that there was a time long ago when the race actually took place in a snowstorm.

Amongst the crowds today were also many members of the aristocracy. There were fine ladies here with their fancy floral dresses, oversized flambouyant and gaudy oversized floral hats and sun parasoles. Gentleman with their fine clothes, tall dark hats, smart dapper tailored suits, fancy waistcoats,cravats and canes. All with there exquisite buggies, led by fine decorated horses and other fancy carriages. Today the place was indeed all that i had imagined it to be and more. There were many artists here with their easils and sketch books painting and drawing the splendid scenes.In many ways i felt naked compared to all the finery around me. My wranger jeans and shirt didnt somehow blend in, it seemed very odd and out of place here. Though it may have been because of my working class background and modernity of my teenage years that made me feel this way.

It was then that i saw him.He looked a very distinguished fellow with his white hat, yellow waistcoat, black cut-away coat, and white trousers. I recognised him as the famous royal rat catcher and king of the gypsies one known as Matthias or Matty" Cooper. He was a member of the group of Romanies who had once camped close to Claremont House home of the young princess Victoria. I made my way through the crowds over to him and fortunately we soon struck up a conversation. For he was more than happy to tell me a little about himself. He told me," When Victoria was queen I was her royal rat catcher"

" At the first hint of rats Queen Victoria would have a servant fetch me and on one occassion i remember i was summoned to Windsor Castle" He continued to tell me his stories.

He said "Whilst there i caught 50 rats and i was so excited that i spread them on the expensive royal carpet."He laughed then continued, "Then Edward, Prince of Wales paid me half a sovereign for my work which was a kings ransom being a lotta money".

He went on to tell me lots more of these stories including "That In 1836, the young princess Victoria had made friends with a family of Gypsies who became the subject of some of her work"""The Gypsy mother of the group was a relative of mine Sarah Cooper. "he said

"Then following their meetings, Victoria showed kindness and concern for the family's welfare". "After the birth of a Gypsy baby Victoria sent food and blankets to the family." "She came to know the extended families of Coopers, Scamps and Smiths well, making regular trips to take clothes and food to their tents, and also sketching and painting them on occasion". He said " I believe that Queen Victoria in her Diaries wrote a lot of good things about the gypsies there" "I must say that through what I have seen of their characters they are a superior set of Gypsies, full of respect, quiet, discerning and full of affection for one another." I believe that she wrote that they were "Such a nice set of Gypsies" "so quiet, so affectionate to one another, so discreet, not at all forward or importune'" "So unlike the gossiping fortune-telling race-Gypsies who turned up out of the blue. Who camped on commons or byways in their bow-topped caravan, grazed horses, sold pegs, perhaps 'tinkering', 'Here today and gone tomorrow', "How often these poor creatures have been falsely accused, cruelly wrong and greatly ill-treated."

Matthias turned to me and proudly said "Us Coopers are often referred to as being "The Windsor Coopers." Matthias was keen to tell me more. " I knew Petulengro, of Borrows' Lavengro very well" he said "And i also knew Charles Leland,"Why he got most of his stuff for his work from me." As he continued i was begining to wish I hadnt approached him. But neverthe less i listened as he continued. He said,"I also taught him to speak our Romany language and lots of stuff about us".

I then thanked him and said i had to go somewheres and was glad to move on around and amongst the huge crowds there.

It was then that i was fortunate and chanced to meet up with "Mr Money bags himself Sir Alfred Munnings the artist. He *who had painted the Gypsies here in his famous work "Derby's Walk". Munnings* was busy gathering some members of gypsy folks together for a painting modelling session. Those amongst them i recognised as members of the Grays,Lees,Stevens,Gregorys and lovedays Munnings was so popular and accepted by these Gypsies. Fortunately I managed to have a word with him in between his painting sessions. And he told me about his life.He said "When i was a young man i used to mix with the fairground Gypsies who ran local fairs near my home" .He continued to tell me. He said "Now im fortunate to have these same families such as the Wingfields as my friends along with Nobby Gray and his wife Charlotte as my models". He continued to tell me in great detail about these folk he knew over the years. "The families that I got to know" he said "Why they had picturesque children, dogs and horses" "The women had somewhere in the back of each caravan, great black hats with ostrich feathers, laid away for gala days, or to be worn when selling baskets or brushes on the road". "Nobody could beat their style of dress, with black silk apron over a full-pleated skirt, a pink or mauve-blouse showing off a tough, lithe figure; strings of red beads, and wonderful earrings glinting under blue-black hair, came into their make-up, and sure enough, if I needed it, the large black hat complete with ostrich feathers was produced and worn". Munnings told of an event he had witnessed which had a great impression on him.He said "One day i was by the "Hen and Chickens" pub at Froyle, we turned, right-handed, over a small stream, finally arriving in a forty-acre pasture, with a fine oak-tree in the middle. Standing along the hedges on each side were caravans of all shapes, sizes and descriptions Romany, bee-hive tents; old Army bell-tents. There were at least two to three hundred souls, men, women and children. not including dogs and horses camped in this pasture". Lurchers and greyhounds lay underneath many a vehicle, travelling families of fowls were making themselves at home around the fences, and smoke from wood fires, shouts of fighting children, and barking of dogs filled the air. "'Never in my life have I been so filled with a desire to work as I was then". "For all my painting experiences, none were so alluring and colourful as those visits spent amongst the Gypsy hop-pickers in Hampshire each September". "More glamour and excitement were packed into those six weeks than a painter could well contend with". "I still have visions of brown faces, black hair, earrings, black hats and black skirts ; of lithe figures of women and children, of men with lurcher dogs and horses of all kinds. I still recall the never-ceasing din around their fires as the sun went down, with blue smoke curing up amongst the trees".

Just as i was to ask him some more anout his paintings I felt a heavy firm hand on my shoulder. There facing me was a huge man of some 6ft three in height and built like an all in wrestler. He must have weighed twenty stone or more. He wore a suit or rather an official uniform black with a stout buckle with a very tall hat on his head. In his hand was a thick wooden black stick or trunchon. The likes of which had never seen before. He looked at me directly, then spoke in a very loud commanding tone. "Now whats your bussiness here young man," he asked. "I have been a watching you" "We Dont want no pick pockets here, or jack the lads here he said" "Seen you for a while,ive been watching you and you look as if your trouble" "Why with your strange appearance, you could be a spiv, dandy or dapper from the east end." He shook his head dissaprovingly and said "dont know what the worlds coming to." He said "I represent the new Metropolitnian constabulary here at Epsom, Im responsible for ensuring theres no malarky or lawbreaking you understand." "Now whats your name and place of residence and employment" he asked. "Whats your business here young man.".

With that, he took out from his pocket a small book and pencil. Then he spoke directly to me once more.Then he said "Well speak up i havnt got all day, i got other more important bussiness to attend to."

I must have looked very suspicious to him with my dress and my long hair and quiff haircut. "Sorry Sir," i replied,"Im just a visitor here ive not been to a race course before," "Ive travelled here from Dorset."

I gave him my Mannings Heath address, my name and my employment. He studied me intently and then proceeded to write my details into his book. He then spoke again, but this time his manner was different and with a more softer tone. "You sound genuine enough, but i cant be too sure see,"so i shall be watching you in future my lad."

With that he walked away into the crowds. I was very relieved to see him go. I turned to where Mr money bags had been. But he was no longer there and nowhere to be seen. No doubt gone in search of more of an audience prepared to listen to his tales or to set up another one of his scenes to paint i thought.

Then i saw her standing close by she was an attractive young woman. She didnt have the trappings of a gypsy, although i saw there were a few standing close by her. I walked over and introduced myself to her.

She said, "I saw you with Alfred just now young man" "Im a close friend of his," "I am Laura Knight", she said "Im an artist too, I rode down here with Alfred earlier, He has introduced me to so many of these people today and now ive been invited by this kind lady Mrs Smith to paint her here on her wagon steps."

"Thats nice" I said. Then i asked her."Have you painted gypsies before"."No" she replied." this will be my first time and a new avenue for me." I looked at the gypsy lady she was refering to and who stood next to her. She definetly looked like a true Romany. She was rather adorable although old and frail. Her hair was still a jetty black, plaited close to her small head,her form was dainty. She was obviously proud of her figure and her well shaped hands and feet.I noticed that neither was the beauty of her features badly marred by her broken nose. Laura Knight turned to the woman and asked her "how did that happen," refering to the gypsies nose. "Me Husband twice" she replied.

So it was that Laura knight painted one of her best portrait. Using one of her largest canvases. Mrs Smith sat for her on her wagon steps wearing her best hat,trimmed with ostrich plumes. Along with long gold earings which dangled from her ears,rows of coloured beads encircle her neck and hang over her gayly patterned shawl. She sat there for what seemed like hours. Then Laura said "Thats it, its finished.".

I walked over and saw the finished oil painting it definetly was a lovely likeness.Laura turned to me and asked "What do you think,do you think she will like it and it will sale." I smiled because i already knew the answer to both.

As the time came for the main horse race the crowds got more dense more noisy and excited. There were many deals going on everywhere with much bartering and handshakes and lots of money exchanges. It sure was some splendid occassion with the sharp colours of the jockeys and the herding of the horses together lined up.

Then they were off and the race was on. The noise was deafening now the race itself had began. I had never known anything like this. With the jokeys on the horses all the horses and riders hurtling around the track along with the frantic waving of papers by the thousands of spectators here. Many were waving their arms in the air shouting out to the horses as they galloped onwards around the track. The atmosphere was explosive as one after another of the horses took their places. Many overtaking others or falling behind on the way to the winners box. Then it was all over.

Then when they passed the line they were invaded by their owners and the press.Then later was the presentations the announcement in the winners area. The winner horse was taken into the winners arena or circle. Here the owner of the winning horse was presented with the prize cup by the Royal family member and the horse received the winners rosette. There was much congragulating and flashing of cameras. The press corresspondents and sports journalist were busy writing out their pieces for the next edition of the Times. All of the gypsies joined in with the celebrations. There was celebrations of dancing and the playing of fiddles castanets and tambourines with the members of the royalty and aristocracy clapping cheering and joining in the merriment it was so splendid. The fairground was noisy and i noticed that the kings were busy on the swing boats and the white girls were still selling their flowers whilst all the fortune telling ladies were busy in their booths.There were evangelical non conformist ministers here too. I saw them all with their mission wagons preaching their word via gospel services with a large crowd of more than than up to 100 Gypsies in attendance. Then i chanced to bump into one known as Gypsy Golias Grey who was as black as the ace of spades. He said that he had spent time on all the old Gypsy encampments and told me of these places and of the folk who lived there. Soon it was getting to dusk and i knew that my day at the races would soon be over. I made my way to one of the many wagon parking areas there and went to the little vardo dream wagon.

CHAPTER SEVEN

THE HEATHER LANDS

Remembering the Canford Gypsies

Do you recall the Gypsies who lived on Canford Heath
there were lots of free wild horses
and a mush who had no teeth
Vardo of all description and washing on the broom
crowds of folki laughing
and the furzes yellow sweet perfume

Do you recall the singing of good queen Caroline
the Sherwood's and the Coopers,
Johnson's in their prime
the dogs were all a yapping
and the tin pan on the yog
You could barter for your living
and buy a fortune for a bob

Each autumn at the fairground
you could watch young Freddie fight
in springtime hear the warbler
and goldfinch all in flight
there were stories in the Echo
with photos on display
with their ancestors buried in St Clements
not half a mile away

Talk was of the rozzers
and the poor old diddyky
warning of the spells and the gypsies eye
there were buck boards and chavvies
barefoot on the ground
with rhododendrons and heather growing all around

Work was in the factories
where Bill Knott sold his vans
the Albion old snake pub with Victor Clapcott
the piano accordion man
Stanley's never bought a round
but Sammy had his two feet on the ground

Granny King walked the roads
oh how I remember her dark Roma tan
Phillips rode the highways and Rogers trucks were cool
you could see the Poole gas works view
and the pool at Waterloo

Arnold's kept horses on a chain
and Sherwood's sold heather
outside Woolworth s high street Poole

Do you recall the gypsies who lived on Canford Heath
they were there many years
afore we were young in teeth
their camps were spread across the grass
their tales were told its true
and John Augustus painted them
years afore me and you

Ray Wills

Where the River Bends

I was born amongst the Gypsies
not far from Canford Heath
I grew up on the heather
where the paths did wind and trees did weep

Where the lizards danced in sunshine
and the sand tickled my feet
where the birch grew on the commons
where John Augustus oft-times slept

Oh the river it did bend there
and the furze did smell so sweet
not far from the Canford Arms
where the willows leaves did weep

Oh the Canfofd Magna highway
with its school for toffs and Kings
the manor house stood proudly
where the Stour river we did swim

Oh the vardo wagon wheels did turn there
where the benders bedded down
high up on the heathers
not far from old Newtown

Oh the brickyards and the viaducts
the steam laundry down the lane
the Turbary common wastelands
where Knobby Whatton made the daisy chains

The folks they danced there daily
and the chimneys were stacked high
high upon the skyline
where you could watch Poole trains steam bye

Ray Wills

Before the Houses

From Bourne valley bottoms along the dirt track
the caravans rumbled to lodge hills and back
through hedges laden with bramble and gorse
lovely chestnuts to nibble with our little horse
there at coy meadows we drank from the streams
little fresh springs and wonders to dream

There were gypsies at Beale's in town today
we l tell you your fortune then be on our way
the village kids saw us and give us the eye
our caravan homes smoked right up to the skies

With rabbits to ferret and hedgehogs to eat
songs around the campfire and family to meet
the wheels rolled there daily and the stars shone at night
there were folks in their glory and clothes to delight

There was food on the table and rugs on the floors
the candles were lit and designs on our doors
the music we played there with accordion Joe's
the songs that we sang were older than dough

There were times which were hard then
and folks who did stray
but we were far wiser than many today
the grass grew so course and the daisies were spread
like creation was labelled for the good and the dead

The Queen of the gypsies was dark and so rare
she had braided long hair and spent days at Poole fair

The wagons were rich and the lamps they were gold
the children danced naked upon their tip toes
the chaffinches sung at the break of the day

as we ambled along with our stories to say
now there's just tarmac and tower park ridge
where once there was magic with old uncle Sid

They lived on the heath then
when the land it was free
before Lord Guest sold it
to build fine houses for thee.

Ray Wills

I woke in the vardo wagon to the sounds of someone singing."If I was a blackbird I would whistle and sing."I recognised the unmistakeable voice of the songstress the famed gypsy Caroline Hughes. She was sat on the steps of her vardo wagon with members of her family gathered around her.

She saw me walking towards her and called out to me in her rich course Romany voice "You do look lost mister."

Before I could reply a familiar voice called out "Its young Raymond," "what you doing this ways mush."

 I recognised the voice and the figure of Johnny Turner a close relative of Caroline's.

Caroline then said "you know him John," John answered "Yes of course he be the artist from down the Mannings,""We used to take him out rabbiting on the lodge hills with my mates Billy and Tony was when he were just a nipper." He laughed then said "we had some real capers in those days with the dogs," " You had the ferrets then didn't you Raymond." "Yes" I replied "I remember." Then Caroline spoke up "We l best make him welcome John." As she gestured to me with her hand. " Come and sit down here with us my Raymond and have a brew."

As I made my way over to the vardo wagon I noticed the welcoming sight of the campfire yog. With its flaming logs and the bricks where sat the large kettle streaming away.

"You should been here earlier Raymond," it was the attractive soft feminine voice of Diana Turner who spoke. I recognised her having seen her at the fortune teller booth at the Dorset steam rally near Blandford on a number of occasions. Diane spoke to me,"We had visitors here from America just now Raymond,famous folks singers," "'was a Seeger and young Ewan Mc Coll from Lancashire up country folki." " They had one those new fangled record machines and says they were recording all our songs."

"Sorry I missed them" I said," " it would been really nice to see them Diane." I looked around the gathering and could not help but see all the kids present. I was surprised to see so many here and of all ages. They were all sat around barefooted and were listening intently to our conversation. Caroline noticed my look and said, "Yeh they be listening as usual," "chavvies they always had their ears cocked up," "they ave rabbits ears" she said and we all laughed. The children saw our looks and heard the comments and laughter. Then they all quickly looked away as if embarrassed, pretending intently to be looking at a variety of kids comics which lay scattered around the area. I asked her "can you tell me a little about your life and the campsites around here". She answered "Well as it be you and our Johnny knows you well my Raymond Il tell you a little I do know."

So it was that Caroline began telling me all about her life. "I'm a principled woman" she said. "I can't read but I tell you I got my knowledge." "I got my little wooden caravan, and I got my children and my thirty-five grandchildren and I love to hear the birds in the morning and get to the copses and woods and set round the old camp-fire."

Caroline then told me, "I met John me husband when i was a Bateman." "Though i was registered as a Frankham at birth,". "We married after the war "she said. " For John was injured then and he spent time in Dorchester hospital." She told me "I was born at the Gallows hill camp ways over in Bere Regis" "All our families including children worked on all the local farms there " she said."We picked potatoes, peas and fruit, pulling sugar beet and went hay making." "We lived in the caravan and in bender tents, we all ate from the land," "rabbits, pheasants and chicken," "With plenty of vegetables cooked on an open fire in a two gallon pot"She said "All our Clothes washing was done from water taken from the stream that once ran all the way through the heath there."

She told me "I first started to go hawking with mother before attending school,that was 'till i was ten year old." "then i went with mother to get a living, " "It was a hard life ,but was the best." " I did all my washing then in a large tub until I was fifty-three years old." "Then I had my accident on the road which made me an invalid, but life is good."

Talking with her and others from the heath I found out much about the histories of most of these encampments and the stories of those who had lived on them all. Encampments were throughout the area and so many with quirky names such as Heavenly Bottom,,Bourne Bottom, Bourne moor, Fancy road,Bourne Hill Camp, Wolsey road,Fox Holes and Cuckoo Bottom. They stretched the whole length of the old Wareham road and caused quite a storm and local reactions amongst residents. These at first were often no more than some mud hut homes then later there were brightly coloured Gypsy caravans.

The heath here was a vast area of open land,though with an abundance of birch,broom, furze and brambles and with heather underfoot. I recognised the terrain as being Canford heath. Situated as it was on the edge of the steep old Wareham road close to Newtown and Oakdale .

I looked around at the vast numbers and varieties of gypsy caravans here and all the other gypsy camps. All scattered in abundance throughout the local common lands, for as long as the eye could see. There were so many Gypsy and Traveller sites here now. All with their familiar array of wagons, benders and top vardos. Some of them no doubt dating back to the mid 1700s. Seems one couldn't go for any distance without stumbling across at least one of them. With the familiar groups of gypsy travelling folks sat around a yog campfire on each one or going about their daily lives. Wherever one walked in this terrain it seemed that one could regularly come upon a range of these. With their swirling wisps of smoke swirling up into the night sky.

Then as I walked the terrain I smelt the familiar cooking from within their pots and heard the sounds of singing and the fiddles playing. Then i met up with Mary Bond who was affectionately known as Queen of the Gypsies. Mary told me." I am the eldest of mums Caroline Hughes's eight children. I was born in Sherborne in a bender tent." "In my childhood me and the rest of our family all worked on farms with mum and dad" "I love cooking, making bacon and meat puddings in my two-gallon pot."She said " I go to the Dorset steam fair each year and also to the Epsom Downs."

She said"I met my husband Harold when he was a dairyman at Blandford and we married there just before the war broke out." "It was in the local parish church and shortly before Harold went to Europe during the Second World War." "Where he fought at Belgium and at Dunkirk."

She said "We travelled with mum and dad in the early days when we first married." "We all travelled to Bridgewater to work on the pea fields and cut sugar beat." "Then me and hubby travelled on to Carter Down and lived in a shepherd's hut for a while. "We went hawking lace, heather, scrap metal, rabbit skins and more in those days". "We travelled as far afield as Winchester." She said "I lost my first child Caroline, she was stillborn, but we have John, Rosie, Lovie, and Jimmy."

She continued to tell me her story. " In later years our son John made a wooden horse drawn vardo which became our home on the side of the road at Wareham. But it caught fire and that's how come we moved here at Canford heath."

After my meet up with Mrs Bond I went on to visit many more camps and many more gypsies at the campsites. I visited the Cuckoo bottom encampment also known as cuckoo lane just off of the old Wareham road. Gypsy Travellers had lived here from as early as the 1800s. I was told that one of the Gypsy ladies who lived there was very popular with local kids as she made toffee apples.

What was interesting and surprising that despite their earthy sometimes muddy surroundings some of these Gypsy encampment contained caravans that were spotlessly clean. With highly polished brass lamps, glass and trinkets inside. Often the gypsy women were to be seen sitting on the vardo van step's outside smoking their clay pipe's. Fox holes was also just off of old Wareham road Newtown. The Gypsy women from here were seen regularly outside the Woolworth s shop in Poole high street on Saturdays selling flowers and lucky heather.

Fancy road was named after Emily Elizabeth Fancy. who was born at Bourne Bottom campsite. Emily's people had a reputation as brick makers and brick labourers, both male and female working at brickyards throughout Dorset. Many of them were originally Quarrymen at Portland making the famous stone for the rebuilding of London's great houses at Westminster and St Paul's cathedral. She Married my great grandfather William Charles Rogers at St Clements church, Newtown, Poole. They lived there along with many others. William built his families brickyards at numerous sites throughout Dorset from monies raised by their smallholding business which was the largest in Newtown. The Rogers were renowned for creating the red Rogers brick which were sold worldwide. Fancy road was also where John Warren and his wife Edith Warren nee Jeff lived. Along with Johnny Turner and his wife Diana who lived there in a bungalow they originally lived in kinson at the "New England" campsite. The Sherwood's lived here. Sidney Sherwood and his 3 sons Frederick,Alfred and Henry were tragically killed here in November 1940 during the second world war when a large bomb fell on their home.

I walked on to the Heavenly bottom site where Betsy Smith spent her childhood. Betsy was one of 11 children of George and Louisa White(nee Crutcher).She was born in a wagon on common heath land which is now part of Queens Park Golf Course in Bournemouth. When she was barely 10 years old her father George passed away. Leaving the family with no income. Betsy s mother chose her to go to Bournemouth Square to sell bunches of white daisies. The first day she went there she sold every bunch. As a result her Mother(Louisa) instructed to carry on doing this every day. So it was that every day she sold all her bunches of flowers in the square. Family legend has it that the Bournemouth Gentry purchased her flowers from her because she was so pretty. It wasn't too long then that her other sisters and cousins followed suit and so that was how the Bournemouth Flower girls were born. Betsy was the longest flower seller amongst all of her relations. She was the best known flower seller of all her family. Betsy married Charles Smith at just 18 years although her marriage certificate says she was 21years old. (It was easier to change ones age on the register then, as no proof of age was required).

Betsy and Charles had nine children, two died in infancy. They had 42 grandchildren. Betsy continued to sell flowers in Bournemouth Square well into her early seventies but she had to stop as a result of a bad fall.

Here I met up with the lovely Jean Hope Matthews and she told me all about her childhood at the Heavenly bottom campsite. Although she had been born in the family vardo by Christchurch railway station.

Jean said. "We moved to Heavenly Bottom from the top of Churchill road which was a place where the fair was held." " I can remember going around the fairground during the day with my brothers Peter and Freddie Carter this fairground was our playground." "We left there later for Heavenly Bottom which was known also as Burgess Field." "To one side of the field was a stream that ran through it. Where many a bucket was filled for various purposes." "At the bottom of the field there was a saw mill or wood yard"." I remember visiting with my mothers cousin Emma Hughes, nee Saunders" she said.

After saying farewell to Jean. I wandered throughout the Rossmore area up and down the hills where the little bus ran to Ashley road which locals called "up on hill."

Then I retraced my steps out onto the Ringwood road at Newtown and crossed the road to where The Terrace was where the Mabeys, Kings and Castles lived. I went through the front gate to the Castes house knocked on the door and was admitted by my cousin George. Then I found my way to the back garden where the jackdaw was still sat in his tree. There in the corner was the vardo dream wagon.

CHAPTER EIGHT

TURBARY RIGHTS

New England Gypsies

I journeyed to New England within birch and heather down
I rode upon a pony there where gypsies bedded down
There was sackcloth on the floor there
clay beneath your feet with gravel on the side walk
and the nicest folks you'd meet

I trod upon the bracken there where the rhododendron grew
there were Dartford warbles singing there not far from old town Poole
the village children gathered there for to crown the gypsy king
there were Whites and Coopers laughing and I heard a blackbird sing

Across from Wallisdown and Bere Cross the gypsy rovers danced
there was music in the air that night when the gypsy lady glanced
she said I had the rose tattoo and I was a lucky fellow
from Alderney to Poole

Ray Wills

Living in New England

I'm living in New England
by the Fern heath valley spruce
where the heather and the brambles roam
across the paths aloof

I'm walking down the same olé tracks
where once our folki roamed
where the Dartford warbler still doth sing
and the sand lizards have their home

I'm sat here reminiscing
of how things used to be
when the travellers lived upon the heath
not far from Alderney

Where the peat they cut in turves so clean
and the blackberry was rich
close by the birch and ferns
where they paddled in the ditch

The Longham walk was rich and free
and the Stour was rushing oer
where the waterworks gave out its roar
and the ponies bridled poor

Where the rich man and the poor man
said prayers down Millhams lane
where the old old church still stands
seems so far away

The gorse was thick and noble
and the fuzz was rich in perfumed flower
where they lived upon the common then
and sold heather and sweet flowers

Where their baskets were so awesome
and the town it clock did chime
where Jeff's and Whites were settled
in the land of gypsy rhyme.

Ray Wills

A Walk on Turbary Common

Went a walking on Turbary heaths
where Dartford Warblers did tweet on peat
i crossed the sandy paths where Gypsies meet
where little chavvies cut their teeth
Not that far from Wally Wack
Kinson mead and old Gulliver's deeds and back
where Augustus John painted the scenes
of young girls hopes and young men's dreams

The winding tracks through heather bounds
where Phillips grazed his horses pounds
whilst Longham bridge did haunts our minds
by lady Wimborne cottages where roads did wind

The hills of lodge and Canford Magna lane
where once stood brickyards and makers then
the winding sandy tracks and Zen
wishing with my pen
to go back and I yen for those times again

Ray Wills

Kinson Ways

On the Ringwood road Saunders built their home of rest
like the Lady Wimbornes cottages
it stood the test
nearby at shoulder of mutton
Augustus John loved to drink
and played with the Bonds and Bests
where all the local gypsies spent their pennies and time away
on those shove halfpenny nights and days

The lodge stood proud up at Wallisdown
afore the council pulled it down
along with the bridge which did did span the Ringwood road
where kings and ladies once it rode

The Lanes run the Bear cross pub
they built the gypsy coffins there by day and night
out of pride and love
not far from Alderney where the family Dove did play

At the Kinson mead the rabbits ran and folks did pray
close by St Andrews church
down Millhams lane at Kinson village way
they played the kingly cricket on the village green each day
Now at the Hub the artists mural sets the scene
where stands the centre for the sick obese and lean

Many a story was told on Turbary land
the Good lord set it out for common folk you understand
they gypsies bartered and bought it all
by gentleman word and the shake of hand
afore the council dammed and drew up their own financial plans

Ray Wills

I had been dreaming once more or had it really been a dream. The wagon was very still now and the dew was on the ground outside I tried to go back to sleep but the bird songs wouldn't let me. So eventually I got myself together. I looked around it was very quiet here I thought. The rabbits were swarming throughout the meadows over the grassy tufts of Millhams Mead in the Kinson village. Darting in and out of their blackberry bramble hedge burrows. Hundreds of them basking in the rich sunlight. All swarming over the land like out of the book Water-ship Down. There was a slight damp mist earlier at dawn today and now in the distance one could hear the familiar calls of a wood pigeon. I spent the rest of the day at Longham a short walk away having lunch at the village inn there. The water reservoir was noisy here by the heavy brick built bridge as I walked the gravel stoned path by the tall water reeds which led from the meads bridge. Here swarms of light blue butterflies were soaring above painting a lovely picture in the clear blue sky. I came to the the meadows by the river Stour where a few gypsy cob horses were busy chewing the long sweet grass. I saw the swans gliding on the river and in the distance there saw a kingfisher siting so proud on a wooden gate. Then my eyes were distracted by the sight of her. She was a young gypsy woman busy wringing out her clothes into the tributary of the river. Her dark complexion and black braided hair made me wonder if she was from the Kings or Cole's gypsy traveller families hereabouts. She wore a pretty thin white and red blouse of trimmed cotton and a long red dress which showed of her figure and dropped very low to cover her ankles, I heard her singing as she worked through her washing, oblivious to my presence. I stood and watched her she looked no more than 18 years of age. Her figure lithe yet very attractive. As she bent forward wringing the clothes out into the stream her blouse revealed some cleavage showing some of the flesh of her young but nicely formed breasts in the hot sunlight. Then she turned her head and she was aware that I had been watching her and called out. "You had a good butchers mush." I smiled at her and and called back "yes thank you."

She gave me a dark knowing look, yet she was trying not to smile. I walked across the meadow towards her trying to avoid the long metal chain of the horse on the way, but still nearly tripping over it . She called out "enjoy your trip" and laughed. "Are you from round here" I asked. "What's it to you" she said "I just wondered," I said.

"Were camped at back of Kinson Mead" she said "lots our folks are there." "Oh" I said "I know some around here got relations" I said "Those your cobs "I asked

She looked up and replied "yes my brothers the Arnold's have them." "Why you interested she asked "I never answered her.

"yes we graze em out here n on the mead"she said "if ya wanna buy some, you have to see Charlie king he's selling them for us".

"No" I said" but I can see they are well cared for though."

Then I proceeded on my way over the bridge to the Inn. At the Inn which was once one of Elliott s farms I was greeted by Mr Budden the new landlord. He asked me "When you came by the river did you see our resident kingfisher he asked." "Yes I did."i said "He looked majestic."

Mr Budden said "Well he's always around here" "Apparently there's a family of them been here for decades" "We are so lucky to have them here and the swans here too."

I sat and talked with him for sometime looking over the river as we sat on the wooden bridge. Then I ate a traditional fish and chips late lunch inside the Inn before setting out for the campsite.

When I walked back over the footpath by the meadow and the bridge. The gypsy girl was gone and the horses had been moved. I made my way back down the gravel track by the tributary. Until I reached the wooden bridge by the Mead. There wasn't anyone around and it was quiet although in the meadow at the rear of the church land there was a parked horse and vardo wagon. Then I saw her, the same gypsy girl, she saw me and waved. I waved back and went on my way hopefully we will meet up another day I thought.

. The Kinson area boasted a strong history with famed smugglers such as Gulliver the local landlord living in his lodge nearby at brook lane East Howe just a stone throw away.

I crossed the wooden bridge, over the small estuary of the river Stour where once the Kaiser fell into the water. It was whilst he had been visiting his cousin at Canford Manor the lovely Lady Wimborne. Fortunately for him his life was saved when two local village boys jumped in the water and pulled him out. Tragically a few days later Germany was at war with Britain. This same bridge would be rebuilt of brick and stone in future years by Italian prisoners of war.

I walked up the Kinson villages church lane then I stopped to pat the horse in the field on my left opposite the church entrance footpath. I knew that at one time the church cemetery itself, stretched over to where I stood and beyond and that under the lane were tombs. Then I walked past the old 11th century St Andrews church grounds on my right. Where the tea smugglers and gypsies were buried. It was oft-times said that the smugglers hid their contraband here in the tombs. For there's still rope makings on the old part tower. Where they pulled up their contraband.

Then on my left I passed the village stream and expanse of grounds of the Pelhams great house. Where the tall Tulip tree a gift from the people of Michigan county of the United states stood and was shedding its leaves.

I walked past the white house where the young Nancy Crutcher and family the Jeff's gypsies lived. They were to include the old lady in her rocking chair with 6 fingers on each hand with Joe, Gert, Walt John, Henry and Job. They took orders for wreaths and baskets and Nancy sold all of her delightful flowers to the villagers. I recalled that She had brought me a bottle of stout at St Andrews for caring for the family grave.

Then I came to the main Wimborne road in the village centre. I crossed it and made my way up the gravelled Poole lane towards the Turbary common lands. I thought of my mother and her friends who as teenagers would cycle here from Alderney to attend the Kinson hairdressers. On my left I went close by the village green where they put the local villains in the stocks. And where the village girls danced around the maypole and Revd. Sharp played cricket with his young talented lads who were chosen to play for England but war made that unlikely. On my right was the village school church where at one time crowds of bare footed gypsy children had descended on the headmistress one cold Monday morning from their encampment at Wallisdown. and wanting to be schooled. Fanny Cole lived in her cottage next door to the Dolphin public house here. Named after Gulliver's fine ship. Fanny ran her coal delivery business from her coal yard there with her pony and cart. She had bought the coal at Poole quay after the death of her husband and delivered coal all around the Newtown area. The Cole's were show people who managed fairgrounds along with a history of work with elephants at circuses. I continued my walk up the village gravel lane then crossed over the Turbary commons where the ferns grew in abundance until at last I came to the gypsy site.

The campsite was in an area of fern heath land, known as New England. An area which had Turbary rights, dating ways back to the Doomsday book of 1000. Which ended with the Enclosure Act. Rights which put an end to the grazing of cattle and the cutting and gathering of peat for fires . A great many Gypsies lived here amongst the silver birch, yellow furze and heather. With their extended families of parents and offspring of chavvies, Grand parents, Elders, cousins and friends.

I strolled onto the campsite where crowds of gypsies were all gathered amongst their many bender homes and tents. It was early evening now the sky was dark and full of stars. With the moon casting its light on our little campsite with its vast array of dwellings. Dwellings which included elaborately designed wooden vardo vans,small wagons, buck boards and trailers of all description. There were many simple crude benders here all made from birch and sacking. Along with shanty dwellings constructed from wood and tin galvanised. Along with a vast number of heavy canvas tents. There were stables for the horses with lots of leather tackle and reins. In the far end of the site was the smithy's forge with all its anvils and tools. Packs of dogs including lurchers,spaniels,greyhounds terriers and Airedale were running free, yapping at every foreign sound. There were chicken runs with pens n houses and with the chickens running free during the day pecking into the ground. With Rhode island reds,white leghorn amongst them. There were light Sussex rooster cock birds who crowed early each morn. But tonight they were all quiet in their wee houses.

    Scattered throughout the site were all manner of large tins and metal containers, a vast variety ironmongery and bedding. Whilst firewood was well stacked in a separate defined section of large logs and wooden beams. Along with well constructed outhouses containing a vast variety of items in storage..

So many of our people had recently joined us in this camp. I looked around the group and noticed that amongst us were a vast number of skilled artisans of all kinds. Included amongst us were those of metal tin craft,ironmongery,smithery,horse and dog breeders and breeders of birds such as miners. There were brick makers,pottery makers,menders of furniture,sharpeners of tools,fairgrounds and show people. Along with pugilist boxers,bike riders,flower girls,tellers of fortune, scrap dealers and general labourers.

They all sat around and near the large fireside yog and I sat down with them and listened as they told their stories. Stories which included those of a Stanley who had gone to live on the Isle of Wight. Of other Stanley's who in large numbers had gone to Dayton in the States with Levi Stanley intending to make a new life for themselves as ranchers. Another told of a Stanley fortuneteller at Rotting Dean, near Brighton. She who was to tell the fortunes of the then Prince of Wales and the German Emperor. As well as her dickerin predicting the fall of the Kaiser. Due to the fact that he mounted his horse incorrectly. As a result she became known as "The Queen of fortune-tellers". I sat and listened as another young dark traveller who told of a close friend who ran a splendid historical race at Weymouth.

Then I heard one of the gathered members shout out. "Hey Sam, tell us about the old days how it was" "Tell us about the chavvies and the noble lords of this land."

To which he answered."Well I could tell you about such as those who came to this land after generations of our people were conscripted as soldiers in foreign wars." "How they were seized by rich merchants as young lads whilst coming out of the Poole pubs. They were sold into slavery on blocks on the docklands of Poole, Bristol, Weymouth and Liverpool." He said "Then they were transported to work on the plantations of the church in the new world". "Whilst other poor souls endured years of imprisonment in Australia after travelling on convict. ships". "Often for petty crimes or unproven acts of theft"."Often than for no more than catching a rabbit on the lords land hereabouts." Another shouted "Hey Sam tell us more them stories." Sam continued his tales."Well you know that in recent years some of our brothers chose to leave for the new world, leaving behind close family members amongst us such as Benjamin here." Pointing to a gypsy sat nearby. "As you know we live within a wider community of gorgas many of whom we know we can trust." "Notably the local artist at Alderney one we know as Sir Gustus. "He who had recently moved into the Lady's Wimbornes cottage there with him using it as his studio." "Yet he himself preferring to live in a caravan in the grounds of that estate, rather than inside the manor itself."

    Samson continued talking to his attentive audience."There were talk that the snobbish Methodist Wesleyan church goers of Newtown were so upset that he had taken the local young pretty Mary gal into his place." "They said he undressed her pretty little body and painted pictures of her naked and sold them off to all to fine gentlemen up in London." "Lord knows what else he supposed to have done," "he got the blame any ways." "Her people lived in one of the many Lady Wimbornes cottages still situated on the Manning s heath.".

CHAPTER NINE

CAMPFIRE NIGHT

Talbot's two sisters

*Where smugglers did haunt and poachers did prey
from the heathlands of Canford to the shores of shell bay
their boots they were worn and the children were poor
with lessons not learned and their manners absurd to the core*

*The gentry were rich then and their houses were grand
but the poor labouring men were rest was not assured
the benevolent sisters took up the cause
through the fine words of Owen and the cross of the lord*

*The village was crafted and the lines they were drawn
with cottages fit for the weary and worn
with stables and farmland so free to transcend
with the community rich in its peoples and blend*

*The primroses grew on the footpaths its true
with the church of St marks close by
the boundaries of Bournemouth n Poole
where the Kinson estate had stretched from Wimborne to Waterloo
still rich in its folklore and the Gypsies ole travelling crew*

*The Talbot community was true to the cause
with our lords ten commandments and its decency laws
though the poor men were rich in their community life
with the strength of the hands and the skills of their knives*

*The school it was set in the woods of the land
where there's heathlands for grazing still free to ole gypsy bands
close by the poor commons of turfs new England's fame
the sisters created a wealth amidst the stoned gravelled lanes*

*Where sweet lodges were plentiful and men knew their places
where the squires were rich and all of the lawbreakers hid of their
face
in woodlands and heathlands where rabbits ran free
the story of Talbot is pure history*

*On the Wallis downs commons and in the rich lanes
where folks grew their crops and the fox ran again
the working men were free to gain the benefits of open land
the gaffers were dedicated and the land was free
where the Talbot two sisters pledged their trust in thee*

Ray Wills

Lavender Fields

They worked out in the lavender fields
amongst the lilac and the downs
where acres of plantations spread
and baskets full were shared around

They took them to the factory
and there their perfume sets were fared
then they sent them on the good railways
the nation to be proud
for the homes of the Victorian Queen and maids

The workers worked the fields and lanes
All the Gypsies and the crew of men
through Corfe Mullen, Broadstone and Upton
in the Dorset town of Poole

Ray Wills

Freedom calls

My thoughts lay scattered on the Gypsy camp
old Calor gas bottles and shiny new lamps
yappy dogs barking out warning sounds
in the night sky stars sparkling all around

Our wagons parked neatly circled and free
horses cobs all a grazing contentedly
nippers playing blind man's buff
old folks chewing baccy and sniffing snuff

Yogs a burning with charcoal remains
flames a roaring just caste a look down the lanes
gal's sat grooming combing their hair
with their fancy skirts and nights spent at the fair

Young men gathered on the green
chavvies talking of boxing scenes
storytellers sat around
cushions scattered upon the ground

old Ma dukkerin she wont change
ell ee your fortunes me dear
love on the Grange

Masters in his lordships domain
lands and properties from fortunes gained
toss of the coin mush then tell me again
bartered contracts spit and handshake
Gypsy's word don't hesitate
whose that standing at the pearly gates
wagons roll down some old lanes
then freedom calls and were off once again

Ray Wills

I sat amongst my people around the yog campfire that night. Gazing into the flames. Watching the sparks from the logs shoot off into the night sky and magically disappear from view.

Most of the Stanley and other families had left years ago for a better life in the new world of America. We had told such stories and our tales, our histories through generations like this.

Those gathered here were a mix of peoples including Gypsy Travellers as well as Show fairground many were folk from far afield. Though many had come to this neck of the woods and heathlands from the nearby vast New forest, Some having lived there in the forest from birth like their peoples before them from ways back in the middle ages. They became known as" The Forest People".

Samson spoke again "We are so very proud that our friend Lady Guest permits us to live here upon the heath common lands."

" They do say that them pretty young Talbot sisters are still busy creating a new village community at Wallis down woods too." "They call it Talbot woods now." "The workers can stay in the cottages built on a plot and each had a well, animal pens and fruit trees." "The residents were charged a rent of between 4 and 5 shillings per week". They have built 7 of these alms houses for the elderly and widowed.""They have provided employment for many traveller families plus areas to graze their horses". "There's a School, Church, Almshouses and Cottages,smallholdings, 6 farms in all"." Each farm covering some 20 acres these containing almshouses, a church and a school."

A tall buxom gypsy girl called Britannia Keets then spoke."Yes"she said "Many of our peoples spend nights drinking at Wallisdown in the Sherwood's place, the Kings Arms Inn, which is close to the Boggs." "We can tether our horses there to the large iron rings which the landlord kindly provides us with on the outside wall of the pub."

She said "I hear tell the young Talbot sisters wont have no drink in their place and no pubs on their land either. For they be known as tee total, they do say, as they just drink tea" everyone laughed at this.

Sampson then continued his talk to those assembled there. "For too long the people of this area of the Howes have suffered from lack of work and as a result all the trappings of poverty." "Out of all the encampments in our part of the world we believe that ours is the most treasured." "Its true that so many our folks be joining us daily from far and wide." "Ever since young Ben Stanley here had joined us." "Though it was sad to hear of his falling out with the Stanley tribe before they departed to the Americas. And the curse was put on him and future generations ,it is all no doubt very worrying." Everyone nodded in agreement.

As usual there were all kinds of rumours going around the encampments at this time. And many visitors from far and wide voiced their many concerns. Often these concerns came with stories of foreign wars and warnings of new land deals. Along with rumours of government proposals to halt our wanderlust. With its life of using stopping places. Stopping places known to us as Atchen tans such places which we had used throughout history. So many with the courtesy of local landowners and of course the farmers during the fruit and crop picking seasons. There was always talk of the gorgas lawmakers and their powers.

Sampson spoke to the group once more. "Their objective is to persuade us to give up our travelling ways and become settled into permanent housing in the settled community like all the rest the gorgas" "They want to get us to pay rent,rates for water and use of the land. To become employed in what they called regular employment, which usually meant unskilled factory work with slave wages."

Then Britannia spoke up" Hey Sam any news on the Hughes family at Corfe Mullen." "Do they still live on the "Downy encampment on Colonel Georges land by the woods there" "Is Caroline still living there and does she still sing all those old songs about the blackbirds." Everyone cheered.

Sam thought about her many questions and concerns then answered her. , "Yes Britannia""Aaron and I visited them just recently." "They are still there and we saw Colonel George and had a pleasant chat with him." "He told us he is keen to employ workers in brick to build a new town on the large heathlands by the Bourne river estuary"" The place which we know as Poole heath." "Colonel George told me that he plans to start work there sometime in the future""And he will need good brick makers,craftsman and labourers for the brickyards he owns". "So will be good diggin, for many of us."

Sampson continued his talk."When we went there the other Sunday there was a huge numbers of gypsies gathered outside of St Herbert's church much larger than normal. Though as you know the church itself is always packed with these local brick workers and their families". "All Gypsies and non conformist Christians" "They had all come from all the many gypsy encampments at Corfe Mullen for the service".

."Their camps are all on Colonel Georges land,There's "happy bottom," , "little Egypt," "Rushcombes Bottom" "Gypsy Pit Field" and Just up the road off the heath from the sea and to the right is Lord Wimbornes "Stoney Down" "Most of them live in these valleys or Bottoms they are all tucked away places". They live in their old mud huts cottages along with their many wagons they all work at the potteries, brick kilns, brick yards and clay pits there." As you know its hard laborious work which is indeed "Good Diggins". All of them are employed by Colonel Georges of George and Harding brickwork company". "They and Lord Wimborne have provided sites on their land over the years which is about three miles of land".

He said "All those living there have common rights by the owners to the bit of land which they had enclosed. Its land which they believe they will never be ejected from".

Then He said "When we were there we met up with John Rogers brick maker and brickyard boss and all his family at brick kiln lane". " John as many you know originally came from hereabouts at Newtown." "John told us of his plans for his future and was waiting to shortly move to the isle of Wight to run a large brick works there." "Whilst there we also met up with Robert Rogers brick maker who also works there along with many of the Morris Oxford,Thornes, Fancys,Rabbetts,Kings,Leeks and Ferret's families". "All the Romany girls still gather baskets of flowers on the lavender farms there in Broadstone". "Other women are still working amongst the hedgerows in search of Elder flowers processed as a beauty product". "We saw them gathering these herbs flowers from the nearby hedgerows to make herbs for all manner of ailments".

I knew that two local men had created the lavender farm with the planting of 60 acres of land. Lavender was most in demand and was a favourite of Queen Victoria and many of the aristocratic fraternity. Dorset lavender bags bottled perfumes were most in demand with pictures of local Dorset scenes. The pictures were the work of John Everett. Who would sit and paint the gypsy workers there amongst their homes scattered on the Corfe heathlands amongst the clay pits. John married his cousin Katherine Everett; They literally lived between these areas, particularly when she Katherine first moved there and she was designing the house. She also lived in one of the huts on the Moors alongside our people and she's planning on building several lovely houses in Broadstone.

I looked into the burning red glint of the fire as Sam told them. "You know years ago the gentry at Corfe Mullen had plantations and labouring slaves working there and many were young Gypsy lads". Sam said "Later years lots of these fellows were shipped out to Newfoundland as apprentices to the slave masters and merchants of the cod industries" "This sort of thing also went on in many areas in Dorset over the years including at Bere Regis under the rich Drax estate, as well as the Framptons, Bonds and others".

The babes and chavvies were tucked up in their beds tonight. It had been a long day and now the folki were enjoying the comradeship of the occasion. Along with the delightful evening,the fire and the starlit night sky. Talk was also of the morrow. The illnesses of the clan and the deals done in town with the bartering of pony sales and at the market place. The evening continued likewise,interrupted only occasionally by the sounds of a concertina small piano accordion. Played superbly by the nimble fingers of one of its members. A local Clapcott family lad and the dancing of the Smith Gal's from the forest. I thought of the others who lived nearby at a very large encampment of Gypsy families on Bankes common at East Howe. Many of its members included families living here over the years. It was now getting very late as I lay listening to the chatter of the many. The moon was full and the sky full of stars.

Then I quietly slipped out of the camp and made my way back to the Kinson village via Poole lane. Eventually arriving at Millhans Mead where the vardo dream wagon was parked. Close to the fuzz bushes and lots of high fern under an oak tree. Overlooking the large pond with tall rushes where a crowd of goldfinch were busily chirping and eating the seeds from a sharp clump of flowered thistle. I made my way into the wagon lit a candle, made some tea and settled down for the night with the Almanac. Before long I fell into a deep sleep.

CHAPTER TEN

GYPSY LANES DIPS AND DALES

At Sugar Knob

At Sugar knob mountain by Monkeys hump lanes
the children kept goats on long iron chains
in Cinders town near Frying pan the children danced
when rabbits ran

The gypsies came to wally wack above high moor
folks had never seen their likes before
their caravans were decked with lace
with polished glass to see your face

There were so many gypsy camps
folks said they travelled from over France
Hemley bottom was home of Kings
Sherwood's and Whites remembering

At Bribery island folks did vote
to keep their homes n keep the quotes
Lady Guest did rent them out
to local lads with digger shag and baccy snout

The upper class Gypsies lived in Wolsey road
the spinning tops were busy that side of the roads
the rag men came with their heavy loads
at least that's the stories what we've been told

Ray Wills

Rossmore Days

We lived in our house wagons upon the Pembrooke road
there were lots of Hopes and James and even Nellie Old
we parked upon old grandmas yard they said we were good as gold
there were lots of folks in the Rossmore hotel and a saw mill down the road

The ringmaster he had a whip and the chavvies they all laughed
we had a lot of fun those days and bathed in old tin baths
there were quarries on the commons then and lots of rabbit pies
the Kings and Warrens ran the lanes and there was a stream a running bye

We lived in our house wagons off of the Rossmore roads
there were lots of divvies around us then
and a Co op divi too
along with newts and toads
we caught the bus to up on hill and walked to see the flicks
there were lots of friendly neighbours then
we had our penny bicycles and no one had a quid
but we were happy on the heath ten playing with our dustbin lids

The Sherwood's they were boxers and the Hurdy Gurdy played
close by the Gypsy campsites with little Wally Cave
the Brixeys and the Rogers, Smalls, Phillips folks and Trent's
accumulator radios and lavender perfume scents

The gal's they had their baskets of flowers for to sell
there were our horses on the heaths then
and turves with lots of peat as well
our chavvies were well behaved
though no shoes upon their feet

The school was down in Kinson village
and was another upon hill
the Branksome warbler sang his song
and the slow was in the still

Ray Wills

Gypsy days and nights

Working at the forge with Reuben and George
sitting around the yog got my handle and my deck of playing
cards
telling tales of long ago Says and wonders drinking sloe
chavvies and babes tales of olden time slaves

In our kingdom and little Egypt home
royal blood horses cobs and Shetland prime to roam
forest days shows and fairs
the carousel turns and the jukebox plays
blue skies and starry nights

The wind of change and fortunes told
and fine wreaths made
flower girls pretty maids
and cousin Mary's dance

Lots of mushes and evil eyes
New England heather lands and old gal's wise
kings and queens tins and pans
sing us another song Gypsy man

Ray Wills

When next I woke from the deep sleep and walked out from the little vardo wagon into the daylight I found myself in an area which was very familiar to me. I recognised it as the Ringwood road at Newtown Poole though all the familiar red bricked houses I had known were no longer here. The Rogers red bricked houses which I knew so well. Gone. Along with the distinctive dark red bricks of the houses clustered together at the bottom of Sea View and Newtown. Where many of the builders and brick makers the Rogers lived side by side as neighbours but rarely spoke to one another. Now these were all absent.

Amongst the furze bushes and brambles now there were just a few thatched cottages leading up to where I knew the Albion pub stood. I then eventually came to the lane of Rossmore on my right. To my left I looked across to where the familiar old Wareham road steep gravel track led to Poole. Then on my right I turned sharply into the Rossmoor lane. I was somewhat surprised by the large sand quarry on my left where a large gathering of bare footed kids were playing. All were busy scrambling and noisily swinging from a rope dangling from the branch of a tall pine tree. I passed by the furze bushes where large golden spiders were busily creating their webs in the early morning cold dew sunlight. I recognised the area as where they would in later years build the Trinidad house. With its small homes for retired folks and where the new labour club would be built. In later years though just a small boy I went on Saturday morning to the pictures at the Parkstone Regal cinema. With crowds of excited children catching the little yellow and brown bus from here at this very spot. A bus packed with kids which would take us through Rossmore through all its highs and lows of all its ups and downs and over the hills. Eventually leading up to Ashley road which we all called "up on the hill" To attend the Saturday morning children matinees at the regal cinema.

The track ahead was sandy and the area was now full of heather and birch trees. I soon came upon what looked like a gypsy camp. Though these dwellings were very basic. Not quite what I expected all consisting of just mainly man made benders and tents. Some of these were dug out deep into the soil itself and supported by wood and sacking as shelters. I passed by this site and as I continued my journey I came across many of these similar camps all very much the same. All were scattered throughout the terrain the area which had little in the way of flat land in many areas were steep hills and was but a multitude of dips and dales. Within acres of heather and in which local Gypsy Travellers lived in their numerous encampments. It seemed that the whole area was but a massive encampment of gypsy travellers. An area which appeared to be rich in clay,gravel and sand pits. I recognised many of these encampments which my family had mentioned to me and were still with heir familiar folk lore names. Frying pan was in a dip south of Herbert avenue by the Rossmore saw mills . Sugar Knob gypsy site was on a hill and the gypsies kept goats here on long metal chains. It was also a favourite playground for local kids being sandy soil they built ingenious camps and underground tunnels here. Cinders Town camp site so named from its many breeze block bungalows. Monkeys Hump camp was by the saw mills an area where in present time now stands a pub called the New Inn. The area was well frequented over the years by Italian musicians. Who played musical organs with monkeys on their shoulders singing popular songs of the day.

Many of the James, Hopes, Jeff's and Crutchers families lived in wagons with their children at Pembrooke road in Rossmore. Along with John Henry Walton known as Jack who was once a circus bareback rider. I was to meet up with Jean Hope who recalled an incident at Rossmore in mid to late August in 1941-2. "When my Mother Lily Hope nee James and I went to visit mums sister who lived in the same road." "As we crossed the road, Mr Tommy Stanley was standing at the gate." "As we passed by he spat at mum." "This wasn't the first time that he'd done this when he saw my mum." You can imagine how mum told this to aunt Ima." "She told her and her husband to confront Mr Stanley."Within minutes there was a blow up going on by the time Mrs Stanley appeared. "Autt Ima said "Take the Whip." (Jeans Uncle Jack was once a bare back horse rider whose family were circus people and the whip was the ringmasters whip). " Aunt Ima used it on Tommy Stanley and he was very lucky she did not take his eye out with it." "By this time neighbours were awakening and had all gathered in the street. It was not very long before the police arrived and restored peace." "The outcome was that everyone was summonsed to attend Poole magistrates court." "The case made the headlines in the local Echo "THEY FOUGHT AT DAWN AT ROSSMORE." "They were all bound over to keep the peace".

Gypsies built their sites here on sites originally intended for buildings and where old buildings, brickyards and potteries had once stood. Our people were desperate for somewhere to live and grateful for any earth beneath us. Though often in desperation had little choice than to encamp in the midst of chaos and filth. Vast number of gypsies were camped in the area often skilled artisans of all kinds. Including those of metal tin craft,ironmongery,smithery,horse and .dog breeders,breeders of birds such as miners,brick makers,pottery makers,menders of furniture,sharpeners of tools,fairgrounds and show people,pugilist boxers,bike riders,flower girls,tellers of fortune, scrap dealers and general labourers. At the nearby higher ground at Sea View for just a penny one could see the many boats at Poole harbour through a spy glass. Or explore the dump opposite the Kinson pottery. It had been an interesting day and as I walked back to the vardo I knew my travels were not over yet. That night I slept well.

CHAPTER ELEVEN

BENEATH THE LODGE HILLS

On the Mannings Heath

They've built a glass office block where the Mannings House once stood
right opposite the brickyard the office and the dump where Bill Knott threw his wood
the gravel roads are gone now replaced by tarmac
along with the heathers the birch and the sacks

The pylons still there though
where the pony was born one bright summers morn
the view to lodge hills where the Gypsies once camped
next to the track where Phillips drew n dug sand

Where the ganders ran free and the hens pecking corn
where the pig sties were wide and the new ones twer born
the cowshed and copper house where granfer made good
the meal and the swill and the smell it was good

With aviaries so big where canaries did sing
close by the thorns where the goldfinch in spring
did sing such a melody that would make your heart sing

from winter to autumn through summers and springs

Oft times the Gypsies travellers did call for a pail
of water to drink and eggs that wed sale
where fruit trees did grow right up to the sky
where springs they were borne and the vardos ran hurriedly bye.

Ray Wills

Goldfinch Days

He was raised at the Mannings where the goldfinch did sing
in long summer months in the thistles from spring
where the orchards were rich in pear trees each fall
where pigs were once kept amidst the good soil

He ran with the dogs there and gave chase to the packs
his schooldays at Branksome and playing of jacks
in wartimes he travelled out to the east
with his rich Dorset speech

On returning to England he drove for a while
from the docklands of Weymouth to the New Forest wilds
he loved to play darts and shove halfpenny too
spending days on the farm and nights out in Poole

His stories were rich in tone and in depth
with his humorous anecdotes and his lengthy oddettes
all his dart throwing visions and quick witted speech
though the birds were his fancy with their feathers all set
with his pigeons and doves but canaries were best

His stories he told to children in rhymes
once upon a time when bees drank the wine
he will be remembered as the storyteller of the heaths
with his unique brand of humour and his rich dialect speech

Every time you hear a Johnny Cash song or a Child's happy laugh
you will see his smile and his unique country ways
it will all come back not forgotten
in those young spring time goldfinch days.

Ray Wills

I woke to find myself in a familiar place. Back at the old Secondry Modern School.

Though this day was just like any other day at the school we were glad to get out. We walked the narrow lane pavements flanked by the two parades of trees. From the schools entrance to the busy Herbert avenue road. The boys on one footpath and girls on the other. Neither the twain should meet, no doubt with eyes of keen prefects watching. But once out we gathered together on the nearby commons as all generations before us no doubt had. The area here was sheltered within tall leafy overhanging silver birch trees lined with pathways of fern and heather banks. With a grassy walk through to Alderney. Once here in this lower ground some of the girls ran to greet and embraced their boyfriends. They couples snogged and the fags were dished out amongst everyone. Usually these were of the cheapest brand woodbines or weights in packs of 5. The talk was of the day and what was being shown at the local flicks in Poole at the Regal. Or at the Amity flea pits or the Regal up on hill at Ashley road. One of the smaller boys just known as mush though a typical wise guy had somehow managed to obtain legally or otherwise some loot. Which most probably had been nicked from his elder brothers bedroom drawer. This consisted of a well hidden bottle of beer to share amongst his mates. Other contraband included a variety of continental juicy nude girly picture magazines which was soon shared around the boys with all manner of saucy gleeful or lewd chatter. Other boys amongst the large group bragged of their daredevil secret illegal rides on their elder brothers motor bike on the Wallisdown road. Others bragged their so called sexual exploits on the heath with the local tart. Though these stories were rarely believed as of having any real facts. Most lived in a dream world trying to live up to the expectations of the others. For to be accepted by their peers as being really with it. The boys in their appearance copied the dress of the latest pop stars. Many sporting tight jeans, imitation leather jackets and winker picker shoes, sporting a quiff hair style or the latest ducks ass. A small amount of lard from their mothers cupboard was used as cream for the hair. With the well advertised popular brylcream being well out of their daily budgets. Though some had some work at the weekends or still had a paper round.

All seemed to chew gum from a cheap penny pack tucked in a tight jeans pocket. The girls wore little in the way of make up although not as much as they'd would have liked as it was frowned on in school. They left that till later on their weekend dates. Their dress was cotton usually flowery like the latest USA sweetheart they admired. Their hair long and stacked high and called a beehive, usually starched with sugar. Some particularly the traveller girls wore large hooped golden earrings. Many of the girls were well developed for their age and were able to get into the pubs out of their area at weekends where they were not known. Those that were not so well developed in womanly form stuffed small cotton wool buds into their bras before going out on the town.

Nowadays the school had the worst reputation in the country for pregnancies. Recently making the front page of the the common man's Sunday bible the News of the World. Though the school was also to gain some prominence notoriety as turning out great pop musicians and a future local girl Ann Sidney as Britain's Miss world. Plus a boys made school organ which was newsworthy. We had endured the day sat through their strict school teaching methods and disciplinarian-ism. As Mr Richards with his reputation for caning boys even a whole class in one go. Often for just a minor offence whilst on a school trip. We were ushered into the school hall believing we were just having a chat. With him standing on a stool or chair to install and dish out the punishment to the tall lanky 14 year old s. With him being short less than 4 ft in height. (A punishment he dished out which it was obvious he relished.) It was an event which made him feel powerful him being a midget of a man, a little Hitler with moustache to match. Then there was killer Rogers whose punishments were legendary. Truancy was a major problem in this school. With its high rate of travellers from the neighbourhood of Rossmore and Alderney area. Many pupils from local gypsy escarpment. The school had in earlier days been officially opened by artist Lucy Kemp Welch who had a history of successfully painting gypsy horses. Particularly so in the new forest.

We were always on the lookout for the "Wallywack Gang" headed by Teddy Jeff. The very thought or mention of them struck terror into our hearts. When I got back to the Mannings that late afternoon Granfer Reg couldn't see his 6 ganders anywhere. He asked me "Go see if you can find them Ray". I went outside and looked on all of the land including the orchard and the road outside. I looked across at Bill Knotts dump, opposite and the nearby brickyard. But the ganders were nowhere to be seen. Then shortly after when I returned to the house there was a knock on the front door. Granfer Reg said "that will be the paper boy with today's echo newspaper Ray" "Go bring it to me Ray."I went to the front porch and took the large paper from out of the post box and brought the large newspaper in and gave it to my Grandfather. I couldn't help noticing the large picture on the front page as grandad opened it out to read. With its large front page photo of geese walking on the highway. The papers bold front page headlines read GANDERS GO A WALKING. The article read that 6 gander geese were seen walking the Ringwood road. It rad that they were stopping traffic and that now they are were in police custody. Will their owner please phone the police station and come to collect them.

I built my huge kite made from large sheets of brown paper; canes, string and a tail of newspaper strips. I flew it at a great height, extending the large roll of string to its base and tying this to a chicken house corner nearby. Such a high flyer caused problems with local aircraft's flying through the terrain from the towns own Hurn Airport. I was told by grandad "Ray You v got to shorten the kites' length of flight", "I've had a telephone call from the Hurn airport to the brickyards little office, opposite our house".

My mothers sister Aunt Macey Castle moved into her new council flat at Rossmoore house and one day I decided to pay her a visit. "Come in my Raymond" she said and opened the door wide for me to enter. "Hi Aunt Mace " I replied "Thought I would pay you a visit to see how your settling in your new council flat. "Yes its lovely" she replied "the council done lovely job." She ushered me through the hall into her lounge. She said "Sit down Raymond make yourself at home" "Good to see you,is everyone alright" I answered her " Yes Aunt Mace " I replied. She smiled and then said "Would you like a cup of tea. "Yes please" I answered, as I sat back on her sofa. Aunt Macey disappeared, shortly after returning with a tray with tea pot and all its accessories. She said"I can use my best new china tea set now,our Brenda bought me" she said. As we drank the tea she asked me about school and where would I work when I left. Then told me all about her kids, my cousins Then she said "You were born on my birthday Raymond."She was always proud of that. "Yes i know" I said." She turned and looked straight at me then said " Leave the tea leaves in the bottom the cups my Raymond" ,"I'm going to show you how to tell fortunes in the tea leaves"

"OK Aunt Mace" I said and then she proceeded to educate me as to the arts of seeing and reading pictures in the leaves.

As I sat there and gained the knowledge my mind went back to earlier childhood times.

How when I was at Arne Avenue at Aunt Mace's home she showed me how to make those paper flowers out of crepe coloured paper. Then she magically crafted beautiful carnations roses within her fingers in minutes showing me how it was done. Snipping their tops with scissors then using hot candle wax on them.

Later that day, I sat in the vardo dream wagon and reflected on my travels and drifted into a deep sleep.

CHAPTER TWELVE

THE GENTLEMENS AFFAIRS

Old Poole Town

They knocked down our homes in olé Poole town
old street lights washing gowns
weathered storms feathered beds duck n down
washboard blues tea chest refrains outside loos mothers pains

They made it rubble bricks and sticks
deserted lanes old men's dicks
they took away our fun n games ropes n skips
hopscotch lanes
gone are the flicks and alleyways
the mothers calls and fathers ways
gone are the tears of yesterdays
the Gypsy reels and the fish and kiddies play
the close knit families of yesterday
the knocker up and the holidays

The olé rag and bone man on his cart
the gas lit streets at night when it was dark
the ball games played upon the walls
mothers corsets, fathers vests, chalk and cheese, Sunday best
they demolished happy days and years of grace
with polished doorsteps smiley face

They took away our alleyways
where our dreams were all displayed and made
moved us all to Rossmore place
Turlin moor and wash your face and know your place
gone are the ways of olé Poole town
the boys and gal's the ups and downs.

Ray Wills

Showman's Days

My fathers a showman a Gypsy by trade
a king of the circus and fairgrounds parade
my mothers a teller of fortune and seers
my brothers kept ponies over the years

My sisters are dancers
the Queens of the shows
in the family histories of long times ago

The chavvies grew strong
whilst us mushes were free
travelling the country
telling the stories of diddle dee dee

My folks worked the land
and the fairgrounds parade
built swing boats and caravans
danced with the blades
we lived by our trades

Our destiny proud
our ways they were strange
to the city brigade

We played on our drums
and accordions too
from Mitchum to Brighton
Blackpool to Glasgow
then Penzance to Poole

Ray Wills

The Last Knocker Upper

*She was the last of the knocker uppers
in the Dorset town of Poole
She was famous in the neighbourhood
amongst wise men and fools
her name was Caroline Cousins
she was the lady with the lantern n pole
every-ones heard of her she was local don't you know*

*She was born in Morden village just outside of Poole
though not registered at birth
She was reared in a labourers cottage
her life was not of worth
It was afore the first great war
when she took up her role of knocker upper
around the quay
But she was nicknamed Granny Cousins
by the workers of the pottery and vine
She worked the streets six days a week
whether weather poor or fine
just to get them up in time*

*She was up well afore the day broke
with her bonnet apron and shawl
you would see her shuffling down the street
in summers and in fall
You could hear her loud knocker upper calls
when the Lady's walking fields
was called the rose walk
folks around here knew her well
you should hear them talk*

*She joined the salvation army
when she was retired
She was loved by the parish
but died poor.*

Ray Wills

I awoke from a disturbed night. I could still hear the sounds of the travellers voice and the wheels on the bumpy roads. When i looked out the little window the street was familiar. It was Poole. It was a cool autumn dark yet starlit evening. Like hundreds of others locals from Poole and the surrounding areas I made my way across the rear of the fire station onto the back water wastelands of Poole. Like the many of our folk for years went down to Poole at the weekends to frequent the pubs on the quay,where they were regulars. It made a welcome recreation after their hard employment in the brick yards and clay pits. In those early days on Saturday nights Gypsies from the Poole and Bournemouth area gathered in Poole. Crowds travelled there from communities like Newtown and frequented all the quayside pubs. Including those from the Kinson parish and many of Canford Heathland campsites.

The noise of the fairground was deafening with the sounds of the organs and the electric motors thumping out. Along with the noisy chatter of the excited crowds and the pop music song belting out an Alma Cogan classic. The bumping cars were busy tonight with screeches of brakes and whines. With the tall lanky dark haired youth jumping from car to car taking fares from eager excited giggling teenage girls. Young courting couples out for the night and the older citizens. Nearby a young pretty Cole gypsy gal was standing at her lucky duck fishing stall, holding on her arm her cane basket. With her large bright gold earrings dangling from her ears she made a distinctive figure in the bright dazzling lights of the fairgrounds many colourful lit up bulbs. With her gaily coloured head scarf covering her dark braided hair and with her long flowing pretty and revealing floral dress. Low cut at the top showing off the delights of her more than ample breasts peeping out from her dress. Much to the delight of the small group of young men onlookers with their fashionable quiff haircuts their dark tight blue jeans and open top high collar shirts.

As I moved through the crowds of fun seekers I soon came to the gaily coloured boxing theatre. Sam and Esther Mckeowen managed this, it was one of the most famous boxing booths in the south of England. They arrived with the fair in November of each year with their troupe of famed boxers including the famous world famous Randolph Turpin. Here many of the local gypsy boxers would join the McKeowen stable and fought in their booths attracting big crowds. Including amongst them was young local gypsies Freddie Mills,Ted Sherwood,Abe Stanley and Teddy Peckham. They were often seen on fairground nights standing together on a platform outside the Mckeowens boxing booth. Many of them went on in later years to become well known nationally and internationally as English, European and World boxing champions. Young Freddie Mills a local Gypsy traveller was born locally in 1919. Given a pair of boxing gloves on his 11th birthday and at just 15 had won his first bout. At 17 he had become the"darling" of the British fight scene. Who would have thought that it was possible that he would in later years go onto become British Commonwealth Light heavyweight Champion, winning the European title and the World Light heavyweight Boxing Championship. Then running a highly successful nightclub, starring in films and TV shows. Then to tragically die of gunshot wounds to the head under a cloud of mystery.

Here were displayed artistic painted figures of athletic bare topped moustached figures of tall bare knuckle boxing kings of another long forgotten age. As if they all were stepping out from another time long ago. Yet all of them displaying their own distinctive Lonsdale brass gold belts around their trouser tops. Close by on a platform stood the handsome figures of young men of the local gypsy boxing fraternity. The Sherwood's, Stanley's, Peckhams and the young Mills boy. Along with the legendary Randolph known as Randy Turpin. All of them showing of their bare topped muscular masculine figures. Onlookers were encouraged to part with their hard earned moneys to enter the booth and be entertained by the great boxers of the age,Whilst others from the crowd more daring were offered the once in a lifetime opportunity to put their boxing skills to work against these local champions. To see who can dare to go three rounds with a local king of boxing and to hopefully gain a fortune, The large billboards sign overhead proclaimed in large bold italic words Mc KEOWENS FAMOUS POOLE TO PENZANCE BOXING BOOTH. The sport of kings.

The crowds were larger now with lots of families. Amongst them there were groups of small excited children scrambling onto the carousels colourful horses. I stood and watched as parents lifted their children onto the horses and showed them how to hold on tight. Then the carousel started its familiar movement and the excited children's waves to their parents smiling and happy. And the parents waving back each time they completed the circuit. It brought back lots of memories to me of days and nights when as a young man i had worked these carousels and the pleasure it had given countless children over the years in all those northern towns and villages.

I remembered those days and nights with affection. Fond memories working with the other fairground workers many of them travellers like my ancestors before. I remembered the gypsy girls I had known during those years. Those i had loved and lost and I wondered where they were now. Were they like me trapped in the gajas world of brick homes and mortgages. Where the freedom of the road and the gypsy life was long gone and now just a memory. I remembered the beautiful Roma Sherwood who I promised to love forever. But war and life had left their mark and meant she had gone gone to a new life in the States. I had last heard that she was in Michigan in a log cabin in the wild woodlands of west branch,living with a welder who sang the blues at country dances. Yes she loved music did Roma. She was a true gypsy dancing gal with her dark eyes and long flowing auburn hair. Yes life had played me many bad hands in cards and like her, the dickerrin had not been good. Just then i felt the light rain on my open shirt,"Yeh typical, its Poole", its part of life here, the autumn nights at the fairgrounds usually brought in the rain. I hurriedly made my way back through the crowds back towards the busy Ringwood road. On the way i recognised Knobby Watton wandering around. As usual the old boy was pushing his old push bike cussing and swearing as he looked for fag ends on the ground and in the gutters. Poor old guy it was said that he was shot up badly fighting away in the war and had returned shell shocked. They said that he went into a mental hospital for a while in WCanford cliffs and they gave him electrical treatment. Obviously it hadn't helped him, poor old guy. Yeh the war years had hit him hard too. There were too many people like him had been affected, or had lost their lives fighting for freedom. I remembered others many of them travellers who i had known as a child. Including one of the gypsy Bakers, George who was an RAF pilot had got shot up, lost an arm and now proudly sported a metal hook replacement. Last time i saw him he was living on the Mannings heath was married and with a hand full of kids. Obviously all grown up now and him and wife were living in a bungalow next door to the Archer family.

Just then i saw a familiar face in the crowds coming in to the fairground. It was old Joe Windas from up north, i wondered what he's doing in this part the country. I remember well Joe and his gypsy family. His people were original Roma travellers who used to go hop picking. They settled down after the war, running a popular second hand clothes shop. Yet still choosing to live in their vardos in the field at the rear of the property. Joe still worked and bred horses and knew most in that business so well. Joe made exquisite miniature vardo toys. Joe had told me a great story about an Irishman who had thought Joe's pictures of these online were the real thing. He travelled across from Ireland to meet Joe and buy what he thought was a real vardo wagon. Until Joe showed him the miniature in the boot of his car. They had a good laugh about it and went back into the pub and drowned their sorrows together. I remembered when Joe and I had spent days out on the Purbeck together at Corfe, Wareham and Swanage. when I gave Joe some local background history of the locality.

Just then a loud familiar Dorset dialect voice boomed out." Hey mush how you doing." I looked around at the direction of the voice and saw the unmistakable figure of the tall travelling local man Fred Bartlett. "Hi Fred" I said "its great to see ya mush, what's on". Fred greeted me with a warm hug, as he brought out his hand for a quick swift smack with mine. He nodded and spoke " I come here every year, as you know mush, I live on the quay,back of the pub." " Its an opportunity for me to meet up and makes a change for me to see how others run things". "See what's new"." Tis also a chance to meet up with many me olé travelling mates from the fairs from ways back". "Many them iv e not seen for a while me Wacker olé zunner". "Course they be show people now bant they and no longer gypsies." He laughed and with a wry smile.

Fred was a local fairground owner with a long family fairground business in the area and with stalls throughout the county. His people with a history going back centuries to the big Bere Regis village fair on the hill there. He spoke, "I was hoping to bump into two your mates down here today, young Frank Cole's and Terry Adams". He said "As you no doubt know. they're looking for some stalls to add to their fairgrounds in the Bournemouth area". I replied, " I've not seen them around tonight but there's so many down here such a big crowd". "But the rains getting heavier and im heading back home Fred ". "See you again soon I hope".Fred replied," Yeh sure mush, guess we l bump into each other no doubt at the Steam rally next year" ."Yeh that's for sure" I said, and i left him amongst the crowd.

When I arrived at the towns main Ringwood road the rain had really got worse. The bus was late as usual,l thought, I was glad to be under the bus shelter. "What you doing here mate, its bit out ta your way ain't it mate".The voice was familiar and the speaker was someone I really didn't want to see. It was Sankey Ward the well known clay pit boss. Who provided work for many of our people in his many clay pits throughout parkstone. The work was hard and poorly paid. He wasn't respected by our folk. He had earned his wealth through the hard labour in long hours by our folk. Them working in hot wet muddy conditions from dawn to dusk. Wheeling barrows of clay over plank boards in and out the kilns, sweating and their muscles aching. He wasn't the best payer either so many complained of his late payments. He saw himself as a righteous self made man. Him being a church lay reader on Sundays. Many local Gypsies worked at Sankey wards clay pits in broom road,including my uncles Bill and Tony Rogers I had often gone with them at weekends when I was a nipper. We would work within the scorching hot kilns. Wheel borrowing loads of clay over the planks in and out of the hot burning kilns. It was a hot task and we came home with our jeans covered in red clay. The Wards were so called religious people yet not of any true Christian merit amongst them and he was the worst of them. Sankey spoke "You want some good diggin man", he said, "you know the work is regular mate I can start you tomorrow at foxholes, if your there for 7 sharp". I replied "No thanks Mr Ward, " I said politely"," I've got a job". Sankey had many clay pits at fox holes and at cuckoo bottom near old Wareham road. Sankey was obviously amused by my answer and laughed sarcastically. He spoke, "Call that a job working with a pony and cart". " There's no future there young man"," That's not a real job no prospects there" he said. "Why ole Edward Frank Phillips and family has that work all nicely sewn up years ago ". He laughed again, then said,"Don't be a dintlo".I was relieved to see the Dorset and Hants double decker bus come into view and pull up at the stop and Sankey board it .Then the rain stopped just like it had started and I decided to walk down to the Poole quay.

When I eventually arrived at the quay there was a large crowd as usual on this late Saturday evening. I noticed that many gypsies were here on the quay tonight. Mixing amongst the many Poole people and the dockers. There was a great many folks drinking at all of the Quayside pubs tonight and it was crowded outside the Jolly Sailor, Lord Nelson and the Crown Hotel in Market Street.

I bought myself a drink at the Lord Nelson and sat on a vacant hard stone seat. Then by late evening the Gypsy traveller drinkers in the Nelson became disorderly and I heard the landlord shout "You better leave these premises gentlemen. I heard the Gypsies challenging the dockers from the pub to join them outside in a fight to settle their differences and see who was the best man . I watched as crowds of local teenager and others gathered to watch this bare knuckle fight. Forming a large ring around these two opponents who were setting about one another. All members of the crowds eagerly waiting to see how the fight evolved. Until one or the other was knocked down or slipped. I noticed that each chap would stand back if the opponent fell from his punch or as a result of his alcohol consumption . Allowing his opponent to get up and carry on if he wished to do so. It was obvious that drink was a major factor here. With one or the other having drunk a lot. And as a result it wasn't expected that the fight would last very long With none being too drunk and dazed to finish. It looked like there would be no serious injuries. I knew that the Gypsies and Dockers often settled their differences in this way by fighting on a fair basis. Watching these bouts tonight and other nights I never saw any suggestion of a gang beating or of anyone using their feet (putting the boot in) or of a glass being used as a weapon. The local Police were not present tonight and it seemed they turned a blind eye to such affairs. As the crowds dispersed and made their separate ways home. I too returned my tankard to the inn and left too. I made my way back up the main street to where my vardo dream wagon was parked All was quiet as I made my way to the vardo dream wagon and settled down for the night.

Silk from the East

I've brought cotton and silk from the east
trinkets and goblets and clanking false teeth
old fathers cut-throat shavers and ladies blue gowns
faded old books you can buy for a crown

I've gambled on horses and I've slept with a few
when times they were hard in a stable or two
the bookies all knew me I was known for my sins
cause i slept with the ladies in a room in the inn
the cradles they rocked n the beds they did too

I was nobody's master n nobody's fool
when the poets all penned
I would dream of those moments again and again
for the words they were all laud and their themes rolled in Zen

The cock it did crow in the farmyard each day
whilst the pastor slept on and the children did play
the forests were thick then and the rivers were clean
pastures a plenty and brooks fit for queens
the potters were plentiful and the milk it was cream
the maidens were well bosomed a sight to be seen

The modern day men with their fine fancy talk
squandered their riches on long maids a walks
the sun shoe so bright then and the moon shone at night
in feather bed lands with just a candle to light

The girls played at hopscotch and the boys kiss n tell
there were pugilist boxers and fairgrounds so swell

with hunchbacks and midgets bearded ladies as well
with peep shows and ventures such sights for to see

I oft times go back there in my memory
to ride on the Ferris and buzz with the bees
those pastimes like sonnets tickles my dream
in those days of the past which were fit for a queen

Ray Wills

    Poole harbour also known as Luxford Lake being 50 miles in circumference. It is a very rich town with handsome buildings. It took the main role as port off of Weymouth and it is recognised as maybe the top port in Britain. It is a great tradeing harbour with very many vessels frequently sailing to the Baltic, Portugal, America, Greenland and Newcastle. Although its emphasise is on its great cod trade with Newfoundland and its export of a great quantity of Portland stone. It is also a safe bathing place too and ranks as a town with southampton.

SLAVES AND MASTERS

The heat of the sun and the scorching G on my brow
the cutting of flesh from the irons and chains
the call of the block mastes echoing refrains
the ships standing by with their sails and their dames

The plantations journeys with their galleys and rum
the price of the slaves and their freedom to come
the echoing and bargaining of the masters with pens
with their waistcoats and breeches and the sun on the decks

The sweat and the pain of the shackles and holds
the cries of the young men and the wails of the old
the watches and purses all to declare a bargain to board
to cries of despair
the handshakes of gentlemen with coins of the dust
black cossetted gypsies with no one to trust

> They marked them with signs on their heads and their breasts
> just because they were different not like the rest
> with rings on their fingers and dark shiny hair
> their music was rich and they went with the fairs
>
> The hurt and the tears and the screech of the gulls
> the histories of mankind without any love
> the trades and the barter and the tragedies blocks
> all for the Lords and their rubies and locks
> bound for far distant journeys and a gypsyies Kushti Bok

Ray Wills

Where was I now. I looked around the place it looked like Poole quay but was very different. The houses were shacks and there were amongst these great pillared homes. These looked Georgian the Inns were still here. I recognised the Ship inn, the Jolly Sailor and another like the Lord Nelson. Lord Nelson was now The Blue Boar. There were stone slabbing foundations here and large stone blocks. It was thronged with people there were large ships Galleon's in the harbour plus heavy horse driven wagons on the quayside with loaded up with nigh 2 hundred weight large sacks of animal feeds corn and molasses. There was a strong smell of salt air and fish. Towards the left of the quay were stalls here a crowd of gypsy women were stripping and gutting cod fish salting them and putting them into jugs. There were a vast variety of newly caught fish here. Mostly cod from the new found land trade. I saw winkles and mussels too. There were large warehouses which I recognised and knew where to become storage for yeatmans and others. The town hall with its steps were still here. Amongst the crowds were sailors easily recognised by their colourful cotton scarves on their heads and around their necks. All busy working loading and unloading the many many ships and boats in the harbour. I watched as young men lined up to sign up for apprentices. Destined to sail on the next boats to the new world and in particular on the new found land ships. The sky was full of squawking sea gulls. I saw a large crowd gathered towards the front of the harbour I recognised men of the cloth those of the church cardinals and others in their black and red clothing. Along with wealthy looking gentlemen wearing fine Georgian hats, long coats, fancy waistcoats and buckled shoes. I stepped a little closer to the gathering it looked like they were auctioning something. As I stepped closer I saw the large stone blocks. I recognised them from the history books as auction blocks. There stood a dark African with a tall black top hat he was obviously the auctioneer. Standing on the blocks were a small number of black and white young men and women. The men were bare chested with short trousers and shoes whilst the women wore simple dresses which showed off their young figures. All were shackled on their legs with iron ball and chains and some had deep cuts marking on their bodies. I heard the auctioneer. He said "come gentlemen here's a bargain, a fine young darky stud from the continent strong and masculine good teeth and the strength of a lion." "Who will offer me a fair price." I heard the taller of the gentleman speak. He said " I offer 10 pounds for there's no fortune in this young rascal he could be more bother than time warrants." The young auctioneer responded "Well then gentleman any offers on this here young beautiful gypsy girl. She's just sixteen a virgin beauty with fine fig**ure l**ovely ripe tits and beautiful firm ass cheeks. She will excel in your bed and satisfy your every need." He said "She will wait on you hand and foot" "Any offers" . There was lots of talk amongst the distinguished looking gentlemen present there and as the auction went on with much interest amongst them particularly in the girl. Then the auctioneer said "Gentleman I have an offer of 20 pounds a small fortune for this girl" "She comes with a pedigree, for her family are well respected local forest people." "She can cook for you , she will make your bed and lay in it for your pleasure." "She can sing, as she has a beautiful voice to send you to sleep with her lullaby's."

    He said "Any more offers gentlemen." The same distinguished looking gentleman spoke again "I offer 30 pounds and that's my limit" said the fine looking man who wore a royal crest on his arm.

    He then raised his voice and said" I am from the Queens counsel I am lord of this manor and I need a good wench, my offer goes without warrant". Then the auctioneer shouted "Sold to the fine gentleman." The man made his way to the blocks and the auctioneer unlocked the girls ankle chains with his key and set her free. The gentleman gave the auctioneer the small bundle of large notes out of his thick fine leather wallet and he swiftly disappeared into the crowd with the girl holding onto his hand tightly.

I reflected on the fact that the term Gentlemen here was closely associated with the Newfound trade from Poole. Its rich merchants were no doubt an essential part of this slave trading. For as Daniel Defoe noted "trade, in England, makes gentlemen"and involvement in the Newfoundland trade was a way of becoming rich and attaining social status.

The crowds here were immense now there was lots of pushing and shoving and the noise of the ships made it even more deafening. I heard the auctioneer shout out. "That's all for today gentlemen same time the morrow with new slaves for the plantations." he said "Good day gentlemen."

I walked to where the Swan Inn was and close by it was a short walk to the church. As I walked through the path to the church I saw there were lots of new graves recently dug in the cemetery. There were no flowers here and the graves stones were few. I read those which were legible and was startled to see the vast majority were recent and of very small young children,many of them were babes and infants. So sad I thought all that wealth and they didn't look after their kids. Starved more than likely. I turned and made my way back to where my vardo was parked.

CHAPTER THIRTEEN

GYPSIES AROUND THE YOG

West Howe Memories

I journeyed back to West Howe many years ago
when winter time was hard with cold wind and freezing snows
i gathered all my memories and stored them in a trunk
composed a poetry book of rhymes to tell one of those times

The ladies rode their bikes to work through Poole lanes dips and dales
there were gypsies on the heath lands there and heather for your luck
the co op grounds were rich in grass and the trees were young and prime
the Canford warbler sang his song and the adders were all fine

The coppice was rich in green and the dew was on the ground
the fairs were rich in didykye and the big show was in town
long before the houses built for Gypsy family
long before the common land was sold for ladies sprees

The goldfinch chirped on fuzz bush thick
and the broom was rich with flower
Arnold's grazed their ponies there
amongst the gorse n flowers and close by the river Stour

the Smugglers arms was tall and proud
and the gaffers took their pride
in Workman's labouring skills
and the young men took their brides

The land was rich in gravel,clay and sand was free
there were many church bells ringing proud on Sundays by the lea
the village children danced their reels and the schoolmaster was strict
they say that Mr George Spicer saved the trees
and Sankey Ward took the bricks

There were many folki around this day
can all recall those days with pride
when Turbary and Kinson were rich in trees and wide
where rabbits ran upon the copse and the zunners went to play
at scrum-ping fruit from Alderney orchard
s and rabbiting with ferrets along the way

The knuckle boxers of Bear Cross showed their skills
like Freddie mills too shay
where Bear cross stood with brotherhood of Guests and family May's

The Crutchers and the Dibbens with Sherwood's and the Whites
played darts and sported game
whilst Jeff's gave chase along the race and hikes
with names handed down with pride of Gypsy clan
and tattooed man
with Giorgio's in disguise

The Dolphin and Pelhams house were then as to today
when St Andrews church stood so prime and good
to while the days away
the stocks and green now paint the scene
where folly true was scorned
whilst village school took kids from Poole
and slates were hard and worn

The twists and turns of kids now born will tell a tale or two
but none can trace the master race
of when West Howe was born for true
the pavilions gone and bowls along

and there's only oak-meads school
where children met with deep regrets
and played by the golden rule.

Ray Wills

West Howe Aristocracy

I hear tell there's an aristocracy
of West Howes rich community
times before the estate was born
afore Dominic Reeves and Lady Wimborne
New England Gypsies maybe were the key
to West Howe life and olde history

Augustus John roamed the great estate
twixt Canford Parish and Kinson lodge gates
where Gypsies families bedded down
in benders bent and promises of the Domesday crown

Where did West Howe end and where and how did it begin
got me searching deep and wondering
from New Forests haunts and and Parkstone camps
Gypsies dwelt in the cold and damp
no houses and no street lamps

Over the years the names i saw
Whites and Coopers Coles and all
the Talbot sisters built the village in Wallisdown
Newfoundland trips from olde Poole town

The boundary lines did get councillors perplexed
the Spicer blossoms and the co op rec
where does Kinson end and the Dartford Warbler peck
who are the characters we should respect

What names to treasure what tales to unfold
stories to treasure humorous and old
families who stayed and those who sailed far away
names to treasure with tales to tell another day

Who are the true aristocracy of the West Howe community
I'm waiting for your answers and cant wait to see

Ray Wills

I heard the sounds of children screams of excitement and the sounds of hammering. This disturbed my sleep and I crawled out of the bed and looked out of the vardo window.

The kids adventure playground at West Howe was busy today with hordes of noisy kids of all ages banging away with their wee hammers creating their little wooden constructed dens out of abandoned scrap timber. I hurriedly washed and dressed and made my way outside The shanty town was very noisy today. There were teenagers congregating outside the play hut and another group sat around the yog campfire in the central area eating what looked like charcoaled potatoes. The adventure was no ordinary playground. For here kids could do more or less as they liked apart from beating one another up. There were a few adults present these were there more as encouragement in play than to act as supervisors. A heavy built tall former one time telegraph pole acted as a wooden tower .With a zip cord assault aerial runway running from it and this seemed to attract another group of dare devils. The playground was established following the success of a holiday play scheme by a local mum assisted by a group of local parents. The estate housed some 2 thousand children per square mile and therefore there was a desperate need for play provision.

The playground site was of course at one time part of the gypsy camp known with great affection as New England. Within the fern and bracken lands of Kinson and, turbary commons. Though the main area of kinson was known to locals as the village and went back to the Doomsday book. The vast majority of the playgrounds hundreds of users were in the main of gypsy traveller origins. Their parents had been housed on the nearby estate after the war years. When there were hundreds of gypsies living in wagons vans and benders on the heath and non gypsies requiring homes. Gypsy travellers families included the Jeff's, who operated trucks as popular builder in the area, The Cole's, Dibbens, Woods, Cruthchers, Sherwood's, Pidgleys and many more were still living in the locality.

I knew that Benjamin Stanley was one of the very first original gypsies here. He had chosen to settle down in the New England gypsy site on the Turbary common. After being disowned by his father and a curse put on him and the future families for the next three generations to follow. His family including brother Levi had emigrated with others many travellers to Dayton USA and became successful ranchers there .

It was said that the vast majority with true gypsy blood had long since left the area moved on, having married or else found work elsewhere. One of the local non gypsy residents of Turbary Dorothy campaigned for to keep the heathlands free of development. She would tell yarns about the true gypsies who once lived across on turbary at the gypsy camp site there . How clean and tidy they were and so friendly and not at all like the modern so called gyppos. Those sort of remarks and more discriminatory comments seemed to be prevalent or quite common amongst many the modern locals. Those who had bought their own council house in the locality. What was very strange was that even some of these with gypsy origins and names joined in with cruel words calling out the likes of didyky. All such terms and derogatory comments which were banded about. Obviously them not wanting to be painted with the same brush as those modern day travellers who left their rubbish behind. After illegally parking up their fancy trailers and taking space on local kids play areas, disused recreation grounds or local common lands. These members of the gypsy fraternity would often join in with the non gypsy crew in condemning the travellers. Often they did it as a means to be accepted and not to be seen as one of them dirty gypsies.

What was particularly interesting and concerning was that many of the non gypsies were themselves involved in fly tipping in the locality. The amount of household rubbish dumped at the rear of the village 11th century church or on the nearby local Millhams Mead was extraordinary. Including hordes of black bags full of household waste,mattresses, fridges. Dumped there by people who were obviously too lazy to take to the nearby council dump. There was also the extraordinary amount of rubbish left in the town centre at weekends and during the towns seaside tourists holiday season. Which cost the local council millions of pounds to clear each year. Yet a few bags of litter left on occasion by some of the travelling gypsies was headline news in the local press. I spent some time on the playground watching the kids happy in their activities before I went back to the vardo and read more of the book Almanac. By the time the playground closed I was ready for a nap and laid back n the bed and dreamed.

CHAPTER FOURTEEN

THE SQUARE AND THE COMPASS

The Square and the Compass

On top of Purbeck where the stone was cold and mean
the travellers and hikers walked the paths of Dorset scenes
where yeomen once were local and the landed Gentry dwelt
where sheep and hills were rich in rhyme and the poets write there still

In the old stoned pub relic where the log fire sparked so free
where the hearth is home to wanderers and folks who are free like me
where Augustus John the artist pictures hung upon the wall
Was next to the old Stone museum where dinosaurs once roared

Where the masons etched their histories and the hills were rich in dew
where the wind blew cold on winter days deep within the hues
the dogs they sat down close to the fire and the drinkers toasted Zen
whilst the olden Dorset folki breathed life into its flames

The sign it swung outside the pub where the chickens all ran free
where stone tables laid their stories for all yet to see
the atmosphere was rich in trust and the poet viewed the scenes
upon the Purbeck hillsides there so close to Halloween

The square and compass told its tales upon the hilly downs
where lovers met and couples kissed their steps left far behind
the cockerel crowed and gave chase to the farmers wench
upon Purbeck hillside
where Hardy's people at one time paid their rent

Ray Wills

Washingtons Ancestral Home

*The ancestors of George Washington resided at the Grange
whilst high above the burrow lay sleeping so high overhead
at the foot of the Purbeck where pigeons did nest*

*Where partridge and peacocks did dance to young maids
in the village of Creech where the brambles were deep
near Warehams proud country with grass walls so steep
where the blossoms grew rich and the zunners did play
not far from the harvests and the making of hay*

*The old house was built of rich Purbeck stone
with the crest of the family in a place they called home
where the USA crest gave birth to the free
where landed young gentry were rooted by sea*

*Few know its history and its fight for the free
the cannons of Cromwell and the royalists pleas
though its grounded in histories we've yet to recall
that the greatest of America was rich in its lore*

*The call to the brave and the crest on the wall
the family mottoes and the days that befall
the village of Creech with its twists and its turns
with its high burrow views so gifted and sworn*

Ray Wills

I was woken by the strong sunlight and the sounds of merrymaking. I looked out of my window and recognised the stony hilly landscape of the Purbeck. And there situated high up on the Purbeck was the Square and the Compass pub at Worth Mattravers. Known as Sqump to its regulars. It was built of rubble stone walls, stone chimney stacks and with a stone stale roof. It is a single story building with an attic. The nearby outbuildings are of a similar construction. The building is built on a T-shape plan;with a two-story wing to the left which extends to the front and rear, which has plastered walls. Inside the pub are two simple rooms with flagstones, a wood burner and basic furniture. There is no bar, instead drinks are served through two serving hatches. In the garden outside the benches and tables are all made of stone. The stone from these local quarries of Portland were first used locally to build the Rufus Castle as early as 1080 or thereabouts. It was in that area where the first quarries were. The chief benefactors of the stone industry were the church .Portland stone became the most used stone in the world. With Christopher Wren using it to rebuild London. Many great cathedrals building throughout the world has been built of it including Westminster Abbey and Buckingham palace. It was notably Dorset's greatest export. Just a few decades earlier there were nearly 800 quarrymen and masons working the stone at Portland.

It was extra busy here today with many customers present for a wedding of a local man and the ale was plentiful. Close by the Worth Mattravers village was home to the many Gypsy quarrymen and stone masons. They of whom etched out a hard living in that arduous employment. It was a common sight to see quarrymen carrying huge heavy stones on their backs to pay for their beer, baccy and and other commodities. At the hatch were the usual regulars stone masons those who had spent hard days amongst the gangs of quarrymen who often were 70 or more in number.

Amongst all those present on this hot summers day so high up on the Purbeck hills was also one Herbert Fall. Herbert was today jumping the broomsticks or sticks in the grounds of the pub with his beloved Sarah. They were following the traditional marriage custom which had been followed for generations in the past both here and elsewhere by the gypsy community. In an area where many barely travelled outside the village in which they were born. I noticed the members of the families of the bride and groom and revellers present were printed on a sheet stuck on the pub wall above the bar.

Names on the list included those of the Falls,Cole's, Major White along with Bert,Les,Fred,Bob and Dicky (Matchups) White, Jimmy Hansford,the Turners, Jimmy Duke,George Connor, Pasha Baker, Leslie George Hinde, George Gyppo Elliott, Les Pepperill, Fred Holley, Dick Croad. Alfie Hart, Ralph Stone,(Yarns) Pearce. William Flew Sampson (Bill) Bert Adams and members of the Bowers families.

Below was another list of families who had been regulars here over the decades I read through the list and saw that so many of them were of gypsy travellers descent. Notably, Bonfield, Bowers,Burt, Coles, Brown,Corbin,Chinchin,Dowling, Hardon, and Harris. All of these man had worked sometime at the nearby Seacombe and Windspit quarries.

Grandfather had also told me that the Bowers were so respected around here due to an old charter which granted them permission to have freedom of the village streets and any horse and wagon traffic had to give way to them.

Today the young Quarryman Herbert Fall had selected as his best man his friend and workmate the local legendary village strongman known as Gyppo Elliott. Elliot was known to have been involved with the lifting of numerous great stones of 7 tons or more. Using what was known as a Portland Jack to lift these great giant stones which were once used for the buildings of the great churches of the land and rich man's mansions.

Amongst those present here today at this joyous occasion was Major White. Him being one of best known of all of the local Gypsy quarrymen. The Major had a splendid war record and after the war he had spent much of his time travelling outside of his home locality to the town of Poole in the area of Branksome. Where rumour has it he had an affair with the wife of the local lord of the manor. He was said to have an ancestry going back a few hundred years.

I recognised amongst the other revellers at the event my grandfather the tall strongman Jim Hansford. Grandad Jim was quite a way from his family home at Newtown in Poole. I had noticed his familiar wagon parked up amongst the others in the nearby meadow land.

The majority of these Quarrymen here today like others previously were taken on as apprentices at the Quarries at just the tender age of 10 years of age. I knew this from grandad Jim who had told me this. Although he was rather proud of the fact that of the hundreds employed as quarrymen in the Dorset county the vast majority came from this little Portland village and surrounding area notably his Hansfords peoples homeland. He had also told us as children that that at one time it was said to be the home of the great Masonic lodge. Which was attended by the most wealthy of merchants and landowners of this area such as those from the Drax and Weld families aristocracy. Hence the pubs name.

Amongst the crowd of family and friends of the happy couple present I recognised the unmistakeable figure of the legendary artist Gustus. The pub being a favourite haunt of the artist.

Inside the pub I went to the hatch and bought my drink and I sat down beside the roaring log fire with my tankard of ale. As I sat down I looked around at the variety of art pictures which hung on the walls. All the work of the artist Augustus John or as all travellers called him Sir Gustus.

I stood up and wandered over to them to have a closer inspection. As I did so my attention was caught by another larger picture on the far wall. It was a picture of the great quarry ship the outward-bound East Indian *Halsewell*. The description below the picture read thus ... It was Purbeck worst shipwreck. The ship was seen foundering on precipitous cliffs below East Man hillside at Winspit. During the severe blizzard of 6 January 1786. The ship sank in a most terrible storm. Taking the lives of 168 persons, including the captain, two of his daughters, two nieces and three other young ladies. With just a handful of 82 surviving. They had survived thanks to the exertion,courage and humanity of the inhabitants and neighbouring quarries, at the imminent risk of loss of their own lives. The quarrymen rescuers were marshalled by a Mr Garland, a stone merchant from Eastington, who sent for vital ropes and tackle. The decency and humanity of the Purbeck stone workers contrasted with the decadence of those from Portland and the Chesil Beach villages, who were notorious for looting, plunder and wrecking. 'True-born Dorset men don't shame their kind-- William Barnes. Of these men who had survived most were terribly bruised, and some had their limbs broken from being dashed on the rocks. The ship was shattered to pieces, and a very small part of her cargo saved. The story provided the inspiration for a novel by Charles Dickens, *The Long Journey*, locally the event lived on in folk memory.

After reading the description I returned to my seat and couldn't help but listen to the excited loud and course conversations of a group of young and attractive gypsy girls nearby who had now sat across from me. All were dressed very similarly in long ankle length colourful cotton white dresses no doubt especially for the occasion. I recognised them as The Lamb sisters who had gained much notoriety in the forests. For their singing dancing and performing in all of the ale houses there and abouts. The sisters sang to huge crowds in all the New Forests Inns. They were famed for wearing very colourfull clothes which were often decorated with very heavy pieces of picture chains, particularly when they had no other jewelry to wear. They no doubt had been especially brought in for the day. With their large gold earrings and silver dangling hand bracelets and many sparkly rings on their fingers they certainly all looked dressed for the part. Then I noticed their castanets and tambourines laying on their table.

Just then my chain of thoughts and observations were broken by a voice of a man standing next to me. "What are you having young man". It was the voice of the cultured educated and tall familiar figure of Sir Gustus who stood over me. He was much younger now, younger than when I had first encountered him on the Mannings heath, when I was just a wee child. I turned to look up at him acknowledged him, smiled and I answered him. " Thank you Sir, I would like a light ale if its OK". He replied "Yes of course young man and a light ale it will be". As he walked off towards the hatch to make the order. I saw the admiring looks at him of the young girls sat at the table opposite all no doubt aware of his other exploits apart from his work. I heard them whisper to one another and one of them said "he be Sir Sir Gustus" and they all giggled.

When John returned with the drinks the sisters had gone. John looked across at their empty table smiled and said "was it something I said" John then left the table returning shortly after with a small leather case. "My violin" he said "i nearly forgot it." "I didn't know that you were a musician" I said. "Yes my father paid for my lessons, but I lost interest after finding my true vocation" he laughed. "You from these parts" he asked "No" I replied, "i am from Parkstones Mannings heath". "Oh yes" he said "that's near me".

He said"I have rented Lady Wimbornes manor at Alderney". "Yes I know" I replied.

"So do you live on the encampment with Gideon Fancy then" he asked. "No" I answered "I live at my grandfathers place that's the mannings house".

"Oh yes I know that place" he replied." I know all the Rogers family well". "He's Emily's son Reg". "The Lady at Canford says good things about him." "He's a master brick maker, isn't he?". "Yes" I answered.

Sir Gustus said "I have recently attended more than a few of these gypsy occasions around here in recent years"

Ten Gustus told me about one of the recent weddings he had attended. " I was at the wedding of Alice White and Stephen Button of Lychett Mattravers recently too". "Do you know" he said "Stephen rode 20 miles on his push bike from his smallholding farm and arrived just in time for the service". "Whilst poor old Alice White, she was dressed in a vivid scarlet and green outfit, and rode to church in a dog cart! splashing her way through floods to get there at the parish church".

"Her and Stephen were married by the local Rector, the Rev. W.G. Newman" " I remember amongst those attending were Maurice White and Robert Hughes". "Robert was the best man that day and he also gave the bride away," "There was many there that day including Robert Wood, Sidney Cooper and tribe who were an old gypsy traveller family. As well as the Benhams " "Mrs Benhams three sons were there too, including Tom who was the 18 year-old acrobat dancer"."Guest of honour at the camp on the hill at Lackington was Mrs Benham" "She was the widow of "Old Ben the uncrowned gypsy king". Sir Gustus continued to relate the events of that particular day to me. He said " It was a lovely wedding though with so many folks from the village there" "To make the occasion more festive, left-over Christmas decorations had been brought from the Post Office, and these were draped on the archway" "Yes", he said I recall that a huge cake was made by the local baker Mr Davies". Sir Gustus then said "After the service, the couple went on ahead of the others, the groom on his bicycle, and his bride by his side on foot" Sir Gustus smiled and continued telling me his story. " Yes I had a few that night at the Green Dragon at Puddletrenthide". "The place was packed out when many more members of the Romany clan arrived to wish the couple happiness."

Then Sir Gustus turned to me and said "Sorry I do go on a bit."

I said "that's OK Sir Gustus, its all so very interesting" "You seem to know a lot of locals." "Yes I supposed I do" he said "ive been out here lots of times over the years." He said "You see those guys standing at the hatch over there . I looked and saw a few young men standing together by the hatch busy chatting. The taller chap with a loud voice was doing most of the talking. Sir Gustus saw my look and said "he's Cecil Durston he's well known around here, he's been a quarryman since a young boy". "He's known throughout these parts as Skylark, due to his accuracy in stone cutting and masonry". Sir Gustas said "see the others there with him are from his gang of masons that's his mates Samuel Stone and Fred Cuttins". "They are all local quarrymen".

Then he asked me. "How you getting back to Parkstone"

"I've my bike" I replied." Gustus spoke "That's a long journey by bike young man." "Why don't you come along with me in my wagon I'm going back to Alderney soon." "You can put the bicycle at the back."

"Well that's very kind of you" I replied." "Drink up and we l have another ale," he said "afore we go." " I want to thank Charlie the proprietor here, its his family business you know."

"Yes I know." I replied, having known the family were actually to operate the pub for very many more years yet. I knew that the pub was built in the 18th century as a pair of cottages before becoming a public house. Then in 1776 it became an alehouse known as the Sloop.' It was said then to have connections to smugglers Harry Payne or Isaac Gulliver. Around 1830 the landlord, Charles Bower, changed its name from the Sloop to the Square and Compass. Because Bowers himself had been a stonemason and the tools used by carpenters and stonemasons were the square and compass. It was bought by the present landlord Charlie Newman.

Sir Gustus looked at me and said "I will just go and order" and he left me thinking to the times I would visit here in the future when the snow and ice was on the ground. When it had a roaring log fire in the hearth and I would sit with brother in law Ron Squires.

I watched out of the window and I saw that the merry wedding crowd were dispersing and making their ways into the pub to order drinks. Amongst them I recognised one fellow from the new forest who looked like he'd had more than a few pints of ale already. I thought how quiet it was on Purbeck in this moment of time. Without the barrage of guns firing on the ranges booming out from the tanks of the Royal Armoured Corp from Lullworth army camp on the Colonel Welds estates.

Just then Gustus returned with the tankards of ale and placed them on the table. "Wel just drink these up and say our goodbyes" he said.

As the merry makers came in I recognised the looks of them. Two young girls from Wareham I could see their likenesses to two of my girl friends.

I sipped my drink and Sir Gustus saw my looks and said "Why you do know them young man". I replied, "not really, they just remind me of some I once knew". I told him of my encounters as a young man with some Wareham girls. One who built herself a play house out of bails of hay with curtains and furniture inside and the other gal. Who courted me and was physically abused by her father who took a leather belt to her regularly such was his discipline.

He laughed and he said " I have been told that by a few that they are different in Wareham" "though I have never painted any", "that is none that I know of" " He said "Though there is few gypsies there camped upon the north walls and lundego."

Sir Gustus then looked at me intently and said."When we go back I want to take the old route the route the old gypsies took" "That is to go by the quarries and through the hills to Dancing

Ledge and beyond to the places Turner himself who is said to be a gypsy, painted" "Then we will go by the Creech manor then on to Stoborough village and then to the quay at Wareham if thats to your liking " "We can have a meal at the Rising Sun Inn there on the quay. "Before we go on to Poole quay if that's to your liking."
    I nodded "Thanks that will be very good" I said.

    But my mind was far away I was thinking of my time on the green grass above the dancing ledge with a Wareham gal I once knew and her laying there naked on the grass in the sunlight.

    When we left the pub and said our goodbyes to the landlord I noticed that most of the gypsy wedding party still remained. Except for the bride and groom who rumour had it were staying overnight at the Black Bear hotel in Wareham.

    Sir Gustus led me to his horse and wagon which was parked in the field close by. He dropped a coin into the tall parish large stoned block with its official metal plaque set aside for payment of parking. I managed to tie my bike up at the rear of his wagon and then got on up at the front with Sir Gustus. His horse was busy eating grass and some vitals from a deep bag Sir Gustus left him. Then I took a look at Sir Gustus wagon it was quite a ramshackle affair not quite what I expected with his seat high up, But it was heavily decorated with picturesque scenes of gypsies dancing and lots of colourfully painted script arty work. Just like a gypsy wagon would be in the romantic period I thought, but not like any I have actually known. Then Sir Gustus shouted to his horse," home boy" and we were on our way down the steep track.

CHAPTER FIFTEEN

THE OLD GYPSIES PURBECK ROUTE

The older route to Purbeck

We took the old route to Purbeck my gypsy friends and I
there was goodies in the vardos and new age caravans so high
we took the Wareham old road again through olde England's domain
we travelled o'er Egdon heath through the Wool and Wareham lanes

There were sights to see each morning scenes of Corfes great hills
twists and turns of Purbeck stone winding rivers mill
pictures of old thatched cottages Creech great Grange and more
Kimmeridge bay in the mornings light and fish upon the shore

The road it gave great pleasure as we looked o'er Swanage bay
with fairgrounds on the hillsides kids and lambs at play
the wheels they did keep turning and the songs we sung were old
like the Romani gypsy language that once our fathers told

There were tanks upon the crossroads where Lawrence once made home
where Hardy walked and wrote his tales and Barnes he once called home
the birds they chirped at daybreak and the deer in Wareham woods
the Sanford lanes were full of Rhodes and the chaffinch chirped so good

The band were full of stories the old uns told a rhyme
of the golden age of gypsy when travelling was in its prime
the trees were full of blossom there were berries on each bush
it was a lovely journey we all said it was so kush-ti

The Worgret track was bumpy as we crossed the bridge again
there were farmers making furrows and chickens in their pens
the rabbits ran through meadows and the blackbird sang its song
memories of Purbeck seemed to go on and on

The gaffers all remember when we cut turves's upon the heath
where old Meg had her cottage there and I once cut my teeth
now the lanes have all been covered with tarmac and man's gain
but the gypsy roads are remembered as we go to Wool again

Ray Wills

The Rising Sun

There was an Inn in Wareham town
they called The Rising Sun
it was on the quay by Wareham bridge
where pretty girls wore their pretty gowns
where farmers sons did sit and drink them down

Where men did sit a drinking ale
and courting all the pretty gal's
its where they longed to live
now brethren and the local chaps
don't do what I have done
spend your nights in simple ways
by Stoborough green
on the fields where rabbits run

The farmers and their daughters fair
did meet with all their comely ways
they courted gal's from Wareham town
they took down
all their loving and their stays
along with all their rights a ways
in the Inn at Wareham town

So listen all you chavvies
don't do what I have done
drank ale and lead a fast old life
with all the comely strays
on the streets of Wareham town

Well their were many daughters fair
and many ladies free
who chanced their luck with gentlemen
down amongst the heathers sweet
just likes you and me

So sisters tell your children and all your pretty gal's
not to do what she had done
give her heart to any gentleman
after drinking ales in the rising sun

Why he kissed her in the dewdrops bare
he kissed her on the ridge hill downs
then he kissed her on the grassy walls
on the streets of Wareham town

Ray Wills

The Winfrith Village

I went down to the village
where the school yard it stands
where children play in summer ays
and lovers all hold hands
I ambled down to Poets lane
and butts close nearby
where roses grow around the thatch
and strangers all passed by

The post office so quaint
with a doorbell that chimes
theres a village postman on his bike
and a poet quoting rhymes
the village church stood on the hill
and the well was set in stone
there are lots of flowers on the footpaths
amidst lots of quaint cute homes

The pigeons close was shelter there
for sparrows all in line
with thrushes singing in the privet bush
next to a ladies washing line

The old school lane it beckoned me
with all its quaint rustic portland stone
were local yokels stopped to chat
all on their own ways home

The water lane was rich in grass
where lovers stopped to kiss at night
and old men would pretend
the carpenters wee cottage
was rustic and with charm
there were lots of dandelions on the banks
and Gypsies selling alms

On Giddy green the children played
games of hopscotch and beggars fool
nearby the cobwebbed cottages
where Nelson met his Waterloo

The badgers brook was rich in life
with people passing by
just close to Wareham town
just a stroll away from Wool

The rambling roses beckoned me
the banks were full of blossoms flower
for every minute spent there
was rich in countless hours

The sun smiled on the village scene
the church bells rang at noon
were life is rich in village charm
and it ended oh so soon

Ray Wills

Wareham Town

In Wareham town long time ago
the winters were bad we had deep snow
the river was frozen n we skated there
then in summer times there was a fair
there was Jackie Lock and Sue Anderson too

Cedric Hughes he rang the bells
at Lady St Mary's he could tell a tale
Chalkie White and Younger Dave
Michael Joseph the one legged Romeo waved
the Beverly sisters and Billy Wright
at the black bear hotel they spent the night

Young David Mellors dad taught at the school
there were saw pits and sand pits too
you could catch the train to Swanage and Poole
Les Hurst was the station master
he worked at Carey camp
he cooked the meals there all the kids took a chance
whilst on Saturday at the corn exchange we held a dance

Ken Samways lived by the walls
where the farm was neat beneath the trees
we fished for minnows on the quay
when we walked to Ridge and Red Cliffs leas

Ray Wills

The horse was galloping well through the winding narrow tracks the hedgerows thick and busy with birdsong. We went up and down old muddy rock strewn tracks where our cartwheels bumped and skidded. There were old abandoned quarries on route here though some were working quarries and with gangs of quarrymen busy with their tools and tackle. On the higher ground the views were magnificent of meadows below with the occasional farmers cottages with wisps of smoke coming from their chimneys. I could see horse led ploughs in the distance and the unmistakable view of the damaged Lady Bankes Castle of Corfe. Which William Cromwell's men had damaged with cannon fire centuries ago. We dropped down into the lower pastures after viewing the Creech Manor house from the Dennis Bonds folly which was built in 1740. Here we could see a magnificent view of the Manor house itself through the folly's pillars and arches. The house surrounded by a tall tree lined copse looked delightful. Its entrance stone over the doorway which i knew was inscribed with the George Washington family insignia. Then we saw the crowd of tall colourful familiar peacock birds with their crowns and tails of splendour. They hurriedly scampered away like some old scullery maids into the meadows as we entered the narrow village lane itself. Our route took us through small villages with just a few thatch cottages of Purbeck stoned dwellings. We weaved our way over old gravel tracks until we dropped down into a wider lane; Which we could see in the distance led to the castle village itself. The castle never changes I thought, but there seemed to be more stone here now than I had known. We passed through the rows of quaint little Purbeck stoned dwellings. No doubt pretty to look at on the outside,but damp within I thought. With no damp course. Having been inside one at these once at the invitation of my friend David Berown and saw the running damp walls. We passed by the Bankes Arms and the winding steep track where the little stream flowed on our right. Then we diverted to Wool as Sir Gustus wanted to take a stroll in Winfrith village. He told me that he loved its quaintness which gave him lots of inspiration for his paintings.

Then we were on a more familiar flat route heading towards the Stoborough village which we swiftly passed by. There were meadows here on both sides of us now with low lying ditches. Within the meadow on my right were herds of cows grazing amongst the reeds and cowslips. Whilst to my left in the far distance was the Rectory white house. Where lambs basked on the front lawns and where regattas were held on market days and fayres. Sir Gustus somehow kept the wagon steady as we manoeuvred avoiding the deep ditch to our left. There had been little traffic on our journey but now it looked busier as we came to the Wareham bridge. I saw the familiar church of St Mary's. Where as a small boy I went with Cedric Hughes early on Sundays mornings to ring the bells. Then in later years where I was confirmed by the Bishop of Salisbury. I thought to those days when Cedric took me to the Wrestling at Weymouth. Where he set up the ring and I sat at the front and watched the matches. Cedric was quite a character dark and popular. It was said that his mother had a gypsy vardo wagon though he didn't talk about his childhood much. He was a regular drinker at The Red lion Inn here in the town square.

During my childhood I had spent a few years living here. Catching minnows on the quayside and lizards on the grassy walls which surrounded the town. There were gypsy families around then the Patemans and the Lovell s who lived out on Purbeck.

My thoughts were broken then as Gustus swung our wagon to the right and into the quay itself finding an empty space in which to park by the bridge.

Gustus spoke, "lets hope that its not busy in the Sun." As we entered the quay I was deep in thought again for it all looked totally different than I knew. The old granary was now still a working granary and not a busy restaurant and there were no metal seats or car parking spaces here now. The Rising Sun Inn was in the far right of the quay tucked away by the little lane which led up to the church. As we entered the Inn I was aware that it was deadly quiet. Its premises were remarkably small of low thick wood beamed roofing and its table were wide and heavy. I thought to myself. They probably would not have room for more than a few dozen customers here at the most. "Not room to swing a cat or was it a pig."

Sir Gustus went to the bar and was talking with the proprietor a Mr Peter Lovell who he seemed to know well. I heard the landlord say. "We bant be busy at all these days Sr Gustus." "I be thinking of giving it up Sir Gustus, cause no trade it does not pay." "Me sons both working down on Samways farm by the east walls and they both be not at all be interested in us here".

Gustus looked at him concerned.

"That's a pity Peter" Gustus said."Have you a menu for my friend and I." " I am parched too."

The landlord smiled."Yes Sir Gustus" "Here you be" as he handed Gustus a small paper. " We got the finest of good ale". "Will that be two full tankards Sir Gustus?" he asked. I heard him and I quickly chipped in,"I'm paying this time Gustus."

The meal was delightful it was of roast duck with the flour for the dumplings from the nearby granary mill itself. With more than ample of locally produced fresh veg and potatoes. We sat and talked for a while about the folks he had painted. Mostly gypsies and that he said that he regretted not having painted in particular the gypsy Mary Stanley in the Forest. He laughed and I understood it was successfully painted by another artist.

I remarked "You met most the great artists and writers haven't you Gustus."

He replied."Yes I have, I have had most of the present day ones stay at my place at Alderney and we have gone out for days around here, mostly in Swanage." he said. "Don't forget I knew lots them before I left London like the Everett's at the Slade's school in London."

Then he looked at me concerning "May I ask you something young man". "Yes of course" I answered. "Why do you dress that way?" I laughed at him, him asking that when he was so unconventional in dress himself. "Well I guess its me" I said "just like you Sir Gustus" "I also get funny looks too,at least we got that in common."

. "Don't You paint at all young man" he asked, "No" I answered "but I was good at drawing as a kid they called me the artist and like you I drew ladies in the nude" .

"Did you get paid by them or sale any of them" he asked " no" I laughed "most didn't know I drew them like that and I got into lots of trouble" "as they were imaginary what they looked like without their clothes" "I guess they were considered rather bit rude but I was just a kid."i said "The teachers at school I know were really secretly very amused."

Gustus laughed out loud. I then told him" I did also sketch a lot of places around about these parts local churches and houses which folks admired."Gustus smiled and said "We have much in common then young man" "Yes much" I said. Though he did not know how much. "Well we must get on" he said, "Dorelia will wonder where I have got to.

" We paid for the meal and said our farewell to the landlord. Then we made our way out to the wagon it was now late afternoon and it was raining.

Just then we were approached by a rather stout elderly man who was obviously annoyed. He stopped Gustus in his tracks and pointing to the wagon said " I do hope your not leaving that contraption here, for this is a respectable community and we don't want any dirty diddy coys riff raff here with their mess" Gustus looked down at the short figure gesturing at the wagon and replied "No were just going Sir" "And no, were not what you say we are."

"That's good then"he said "Well be off with you then or il get the law on you".

And as he walked away Gustus turned to me and said,"You can see what its coming too cant you. " "Why soon there wont be any stopping places any blade of grass left for gypsies anywhere" "Or in fact any bit of land where they can live peacefully." I thought of William Barnes the Dorset poet and prophet from hereabouts who had himself said the very same words in those days. Then Gustus said,"Why they l want to send them back to wherever they come from""whether that be Egypt or India". As he uttered that sentence I thought to myself, " yes your so right, that was so prophetic,you don't know how right you are Sir Gustus". As I climbed up onto the wagon patting the old horse on the way.

As we continued our way I noticed that Gustus was deep in thought. I turned to him and asked him "your very quiet Sir." "Yes im sorry got a lot on my mind" he said. Then he told me. " As you know I live at the Alderney Manor thanks to my artist friend

Kathleen Everett who introduced me to the Lady" "You mean Lady Wimborne don't you Gustus". "Yes that's right" he said. "She had built lots of fine cottages for all those people who worked on her estates". Yes I know" i answered. He continued,"Well as you know I love to paint the young ladies as well as the gypsies and those in high ranking"

"I'm going back to Alderney today as I promised a family I got to know well that I would love to paint a portrait of their young daughter" he said "At first they were not too keen on the idea as they'd been told of my many affairs and encounters with my lady models" "Their daughter Mary is a beautiful young lady with lovely figure long flowing hair and I just want to paint her" "nothing more than that you understand" "Their not a wealthy family, her father works on lady Wimbornes estate,where he tends her horses there at Canford stables" "What I am offering as payment of their daughters sitting for a picture would be a small fortune to them" "My Dorelia has agreed and would be present whilst I worked on Mary's picture you understand, so all would be correct and in good Christian ways." "So its tonight Mary will take her first sitting for me" "I have arranged to collect her early evening from her home and take her to my studio."

I asked "where does she live." Gustus replied,"She lives in one of the pretty Lady Wimborne cottages, just on the top of the hill at Mannings heath" "Just above the delightful Heather View cottage where the young Rogers family lived." I smiled. For I knew that those people who lived in these cottages were the Gears and the Clappcotts and a young painter lodger name of Henry. As we continued our journey towards Poole the rain had eased off and the sky was cloudless. There were many cars on the roads now though few compared to those in the future.

As we entered the Quay at Poole, Gustus turned to me and said."Shall we have one for the road" "No thanks" I replied "not for me Sir Gustus."

"Well I must have a few jugs at the Nelson before I go and maybe play some shove halfpenny with the locals."he said. I nodded " il just lay down in the back of the vardo here if that's alright." I said . For I was feeling tired now.

"Yes of course" Gustus said. Then he called to the horse to stop the wagon. " I wont be too long" he said, as he jumped down to the ground.

Then as he left I found my way to the rear of the wagon and laid down on the soft mattress, fancy pillows and cushions there and soon I dropped off to sleep.

CHAPTER SIXTEEN

AT HEATHER VIEW

Heather View

How I remember days at heather view
with views across to Waterloo
where Marion Archer and i did play
upon the swing above the hay

The cottage stood upon the hill
with rambling roses around the window sills
the bricks were painted red and white
with door of green and stable light

The furze was sharp and the broom was rich
where ponies grazed and willows pitched
the gravel road was rich in time
where Augustus painted the house so fine

The common lands stretched to Magna road
with foxes lair's and newts and toads
the rabbits played upon the downs
where gypsy folk were bedded down

The Archers lived at Heather view
where Sankey Ward had chimney new
where clay was rich and sand was prime
where horses grazed most of the time

The Phillips lorries drove by each day
where kids would chase and run n play
the daisy banks were green and rich
with buttercups along the ditch

*The common hedges were thick with dew
where golden spiders crafted webs so true
where lizards squirmed and adders chased
amongst the heathers rich in bloom and face*

*The days were long and sunny too
with views across to the town of Poole
where train did chuff and spout did steam
from lights of town and birch tree leans*

*Those days have gone and where we played
replaced by speed of moneys made
where factories stand and office space
lost to the pride of our parade*

Ray Wills

Brick maker

My granfer was a master brick maker
he worked the kilns and downs
life was hard amongst the shifts then
working for a crown

The landed gentry owned the land
whilst the common people prayed
the Gypsies worked the pits and clay
all the land around night and day

Amongst the vardos and the benders
the huts with wagons strong
the chavvies running through the mire
with the sweet lavender growing wild

The hours were long in brickyards then
when families were close
with the donkeys and the ponies
where the bricks sailed from the coast

My granfer was a brick maker
his family owned the yards
red bricks to build the Bournemouth town
with sand pits close by and around
they worked the kilns and clay pits then
with Gypsies standing by

Ray Wills

The old clay cutters

There were gangs of clay cutters on Mitchell's site
cutting clay by day and night
the work was tiresome and the hours long
but they we're mean and they were strong

On Alder hills they dug the quarry
their kids to feed and waif's they'd married
the Talbot land was rich in clay
with a good days work for a poor man's pay

The brickyards stretched across the land
from Wareham road to Turbarys sands
Old Meg the gypsy lived in her cottage on the heath
where tinkers blessed the turves's so deep

To cut their turves's was to survive
in winter time when love was wild
the warblers sang their songs for free
whilst the adders and lizards squirmed
beneath birch trees

The common land was fit to roam
with gypsy vendors with high curved domes
the sacks were plentiful on the ground
where fir cones dropped and beggars scrounged

The Talbot Sisters heard their pleas
the working men and amidst poor widows leas
they built a village to be proud
like the Winton soil the land was loud

The Whites and Rogers created bricks
with chimneys tall and windows thick
where the common man used land so free
to build their homes in Alderney

Ray Wills

On Wally Wack

On Saturday Eve we left the confines of our heather camp
with our horse led wagons we did advance
up to the windy straights of Wallisdown laments
leaving behind the families Phillips and Trent's

All our loyal band of Gypsy crew
on the border lands of bourne and Poole
here in the forecourt of an Inn abode kings arms
where of folks in winter to spring our tales were told

Where bluebells filled the nearby woodlands Alder leas
with scents so fresh to comfort thee
there we tethered our horses cobs and all
tethered to the iron rings there out of view to stall

Whilst we entered in the doors of the local Inn
with greetings of a merry landlord Sherwood glad welcoming
it was here we sat and shared a brew
of the finest ales this side of Poole

Where straws were laid out upon the floor
we sat and joked with Molly Doe and Kenny Small
just close to the woods where sisters Talbot
bought a land to build a dream they sought
and planned well within their means

Our wagons rolled upon the Wally wacks
where our folks grew rich in clay and bricks and commons sacks
we sang our songs and told our tales
and drank to the lords no matter what

For we were happy as could be
on the nights out on the town so merrily

Ray Wills

When I awoke I could smell the broom and the sweet yellow flowers scents of the yellow dust of the furze bushes once again. Here I was back once again a wee nipper on the Mannings heath road. Playing in the clearing of broom with my dog Rusty the Airedale. It was quiet here with just bird song for company. Then I saw him coming towards me down the hill. Of all the larger than life characters who frequented the numerous schools, circles and salons of the literary and art world. An early new age traveller and the top portrait painter of his generation.

He was a strange looking elderly man shuffling towards me down the steep gravel road. As he got closer I saw he wore the strangest of clothes I had ever seen. Not dressed at all like my grandfather and my two uncles or any of the other grown ups men I knew. His clothes were long dark and shabby looking he wore the largest of hats so wide and fancy. His features were dark and foreboding with a long black beard and curled moustache. As he got nearer I saw he was carrying a wooden contraption the like of which I had never seen before. Along with a wood box and a stool. What a strange man I thought. As he approached me and as he got near I saw his eyes though they were kind and clear blue. And then he smiled which made me feel at ease. Then he spoke "Good morning young master. " His voice was different from those of my people, posh like. When he reached to where I stood he stopped. Then he proceeded to set up his contraption in the clearing. I saw now that this was some kind of board with legs and it had a canvas board mounted upon it. He opened the wooden box and surprisingly it contained a variety of small tubes the like of which I had never seen before. Along with a variety of small fancy brushes of all sizes, a charcoal, pencils and what looked like miniature bottles of turpentine.

It all looked very weird. He smiled at me as he worked then he spoke. "I expect your not accustomed to see an artist at his work my son". I just stared and stared in astonishment. I was so amazed by this magician or wizard. He looked just like he had stepped out of one my little story books. "No" I said "I ain't mister". Like all kids at my age I was inquisitive in fact perhaps because of my big ears I was known as rabbits ears.

"What's it for mister" I asked. He replied, "Its my work, my young master and your about to see an artist at his work". He smiled at me and prepared to open his little tubes and I watched as he spread snatches of it out onto his wee board. They were all of many rich colours and of substance as I have never ever seen. And not at all like my little water colour paint set at home. "These are called oils"! he said "And I use them to paint my pictures". I looked and him and said "What pictures do you paint mister". He smiled and replied ." Why all kinds, I paint people, famous some of them and gypsies." " why they are my speciality little gypsy boys like you". "You are gypsy are you not"he said.

But I didn't answer him being unaware of what a gypsy was any ways. "What you painting now mister" I asked. He replied, "Well my inquisitive wee friend I am about to set up and start to paint this exquisite delightful cottage here". With the index finger of his right hand pointing towards our one time family home Heather view, which stood facing us on the edge of the gravel road. The Heather view looked so pretty today I thought with the sun shining on its red and white brickwork. "That's the lady's house" I said "hope you got per missn to paint it "I asked. "Why" , "Yes of course" he replied" I have specific permission from The lady Wimborne herself, as she instructed me to paint it for her, and your folks know". "I believe they rent from her". "Yeh my granfer does" I replied. He spoke again. "Such pretty red rose bushes growing up its walls and delightful bay windows the like iv e not seen before" he said.

I said "my granfer made the bricks for they be Rogers bricks". He replied "Yes so I am told, they are the best" he answered. Just then I heard my Grans loud voice shout out calling out to me from the road below, "Boy where are you Raymond".

I turned to him and hurriedly waved goodbye "I gotta go mister " I said "bye". I called out to my my dog,"Rusty here girl" Rusty ran to me and we followed as we made our way down the gravel hill to the Mannings. The man looked at me smiled and said "bye young master see you again." I ran off down the gravel stone road till I reached the house.

When I arrived at the Mannings, my Gran was by the main door waiting for me and asked "why are you late,"

I told her about the man. It was obvious that she wasn't happy and she was annoyed with me for some reason. She spoke angrily. " You keep a ways from him you hear me, he's a dirty old man chases women." She spoke again directly at me. "He's, no good you hear me Ray."

"Yes Gran" i said and I went up the stairs to the bathroom and washed my grubby hands ready for tea.

After the infant boy had gone Gustus sat in the clearing and reflected on his life. Whilst putting onto the canvas the initial background of the picture.

It was quite a few years since he had lived nearby at his Alderney manor studio. Much had happened since those days. His thoughts were of arriving at Alderney in the wagon with Dorelia and the family all singing back in 1911. He remembered the crazy days and nights at the manor. The parties he held there which seemed to last forever. All the many folks from the art and literary world who visited him. Many often staying for weeks,months or even years. With some staying in the blue and yellow Gypsy caravans and at parties they stayed in gypsy tents or alfresco in the orchard.

Gustus had painted and sketched the children and guests then. Them taking part in afternoon jazz sessions - the tango was his speciality. The Manor then covered acres of land with a lake and the Johns had acquired all the trappings of a back to the land community. With cows, saddleback pigs, donkeys, New Forest ponies, carthorses, cats & dogs, bees doves and a' monkey.

He thought how much he loved his regular trips to all the local pubs including the Bear cross, Shoulder of mutton and Kngs arms. To play darts and shove halfpenny as well as in regular card schools. How much he had enjoyed those evenings with all the locals and gypsies. He also loved being in the Sea view hotel at Parkstone and especially the Lord Nelson at Poole.

He thought back to that very first meeting with the Lady. He had been introduced to her by his friends the Everett's. Katherine and John. Katherine Everett had described to him the Alderney manor. As *'an unusually attractive house built by an eccentric Frenchman".* "With its Gothic windows and a castellated parapet with additional cottages and a round walled garden".

Lady Wimborne must have admired me and my work he thought. For she allowed me to rent the Manor for the ridiculous sum of just £50 a year. He admired her eloquence and her kindnesses to the locals and particularly the gypsies. Gustus had had many women in his life, women of all shapes and sizes, beautiful and not so beautiful. But she was above all else the very best of them though he had never made any advances towards her. Her being a married lady of great esteem. Or even offered to paint her portrait or like so many other ladies he painted, never her in the nude.

He reflected and remembered all those women he'd painted over the years in many evocative sexually alluring positions and later many of whom he had made love to. He smiled to himself in his thought and spoke out loud "Yeh I have seen a few sights in my time ,though the female form was always so delightful to paint, or to make love to". He thought of all the gypsy gal's he had known over the years. Amongst them the great folk singers and dancers. Those he had shared a bender with on cold frosty nights on the heaths. After siting around the yog campfire with their family. All singing his songs and him listening to their many Says. He thought of all the local young gal's from this area in particular. He remembered when he had painted in the nude a young local girl Mary who lived on the Manning's Heath road in one of Lady Wimbornes estate workers cottages. He recalled how it caused quite a scandal at that time within the local Newtown area church going community. Those who he'd painted and the storm it brought from the local members of the church. All church going people with strict moral codes and the promise of hell fire and damnation. He knew he was gossip. The talk was of him having made love to so many young virgins making them pregnant,hundreds they said. He knew this was a total fabrication, exaggerated out of all proportion. He knew of a handful of those he had made love to and had paid their families handsomely for such pleasures. He had visited the families and his illegitimate love children regularly resulting from these encounters ensuring their welfare.

Gustus thought back to his youth and how he first became interested in the gypsy life. When having a break from his studies in London's Slade school of art whilst on a walking trip around Pembrokeshire he had come across some Irish tinkers. Then in later years when he made a great friendship with John Samson their visit to cabbage hill gypsy camp. Samson a self taught Romany scholar and university lecturer who had opened Gustus eyes to an awakening of the rich gypsy culture language and lifestyle. Gustus was won over the Rai was a gentleman..

Though it was a fact that in his own childhood both his father and grandfather warned him off of ever having anything to do with the gypsies. His father had warned all of his children that if they walked abroad on market days,they would be kidnapped by Gypsies. Spirited away in their caravans no one knows where. Augustus had longed to be someone other than his fathers son. This had a great bearing on John and as a result John spent much of his life painting and etching the local Gypsies and was regarded with much respect by both the Gypsy community and the wider art world. However throughout his life from the time of the encounter and the influence of Samson. John had searched out their gypsy encampments wherever he went. Often travelling in his own horse drawn wagons. He saw these folk as having true freedom and a way of life like none other in richness. He considered them true anti capitalists, rebelling against the capitalist society of the day. Fortunately they the gypsies likewise came to see him as a true friend and honorary gypsy calling him Sir Gustas.

Gustus recalled painting one of his most admired works "The Mumper's Child" a local traveller child who lived at one of the gypsy camps at Alderney. John thought of those days and how he was perhaps the best-known artist in Britain at the time. Being the peak of his artistic career. when he was much in demand to paint everyone and they all clambered for his attention then. As well as friends, like Ottoline Morrell and W. B. Yeats he had painted Lloyd George, Ramsay MacDonald & Winston Churchill. He recalled when he had painted famous of all Dorset's residents T.E Lawrence and Thomas Hardy. John smiled to himself as he recalled how Hardy on seeing his portrait painted by him in 1923 remarked. "I don't know if that's how I look, but that's how I feel."

Gustus recalled days at Swanage with his sister Gwen and his friend the painter Charles Conder at the masons pub on Purbeck hills. Attending those grand weddings of jump the sticks of the gypsy quarrymen.. Gustus thought that it was a great pity that Charles took to drink and women of bad sexual character then caught the pox and died so young. For there was no doubt that Charles art work of Swanage and its people was wonderful.

In those early days at Alderney Gustus children's had been looked after by his sisters Rose & Lily. Rose and Lily rode round the neighbourhood in a wicker pony and trap known as 'the Hallelujah Chariot'. They were prominent in the local Salvation Army and followers of the Quakers .

Gustus children were full of mischief and freedom loving in those early days,They ran wild over the heathland and through the Alderney woods & bathed naked in the large pond. Playing in the local broom road Dorset Brick company's brickyard and the Rogers families brickyard where Reginald Rogers worked as a brick maker and playing at the many Edward Frank Phillips sand and gravel pits. Those were good times Gustus thought as he added some more turpentine to his oils and then continued to work on his painting of the cottage.

Gustus had loved living at Alderney but never regretted moving to his present home in the forest at Fryern Court, Fordingbridge. Which was a 14th century friary turned farmhouse. He thought it ideal and had become a stopping-off point for artists travelling to the West Country from London. His present home as before at Alderney had developed into an open house, but it was not as a commune as Alderney was. In the less hectic lifestyle at Fryern he had entered the twilight of his artistic career. He enjoyed pestering the MPs these days on behalf of Gypsy & travellers' rights and was greatly honoured to be elected president of the Gypsy Law Society. He was an anarchist at heart, a philosopher and a social libertarian though an eccentric. He recalled speaking out against hedges. 'Hedges are miniature frontiers when serving as bulkheads, not windscreens" he would say. "Hedges as bulkheads dividing up the Common Land all should come down, for they represent and enclose stolen property".

He spent occasional trips abroad or up to London where he still enjoyed a drink. Just as he had here in the past at the Bere Cross and the Shoulder of Mutton. He was still proud of the fact that he could still out-drink, out-party and out-flirt his considerably younger companions. He still considered himself a ladies man for his romancing and affairs had continued. He had numerous affairs with many women from the aristocratic world, including Ian Flemings mother. Though gypsies were his life and he often went for a continental tour in search of gypsy camps or new lovers.

He recalled striking up a friendship with Lord Beaverbrook which enabled him to obtain a commission in the Canadian Army. He laughed to himself how he was permitted to paint what he liked on the Western Front. How he was also allowed to grow his beard. Him being the only officer in the Allied forces, except for King George V, to have one. H e had always been outspoken hot tempered and often got into fights After two months in France, he nearly got court-martial after he got into a street fight.

Gustus had made good progress on his painting of the cottage now and he was quite pleased with it. He was just about to clear up and put his oils and his easel away when he heard a familiar voice. Looking up the gravel road he saw the white van and the unmistakeable figure of the gypsy Basil Burton. Basil said "Hows it going Sir Gustus". Gustus smiled and answered "very well its good to see you what you doing these parts Basil".

"I work down there" he said pointing down the road. . "I be the new warden at the camp there at the camp" he said "I work for Dorset county council now". Gustus looked surprised and said "You mean that you actually been employed by them, well I never". "i would never believed it them gorgas employing a gypsy"

Basil said "Well they did and its a good number, though some the new intake there are trouble".

"Who are they" Gustus asked "anyone I know".

"They are not from these parts not our Romany"Basil replied "They are Irish travellers and diddykys who work on tarmacking and scrap metal". "Some of them are not really genuine gypsies, but well we had to take em in.".

Gustus smiled and said " Not an easy job that Basil ,I don't envy you". Basil replied "But its a good job and there's many good people there including the Bonds and Sherwood's amongst them" "Any ways Reg is next door at the Mannings house if I wanna yarn and cuppa."

Gustus nodded his head and Basil asked." Do you see the Sherwood's the new people here Sir Gustus" He was referring to the new family living in the cottage.

Gustus answered"No not seen anyone today." "Apart a wee nipper from Regs place."

Basil said "Oh that l be his grandson Raymond he been brought up by Reg n Alice". Gustus nodded and answered " He asked a lot questions".

Basil said "Yeah rabbits ears" he laughed "He's Bill Hansfords boy old Bills a cripple these days had a bad fall. He saw Gustus easel and asked him "What you painting Gustus".

Gustus replied" Its a picture of the cottage the Lady herself asked me to paint". Basil wandered closer and gave the picture a good look over and then said "Your making a good job that it sure is a nice picture of the place." "Yes, thanks Basil" " I better get going soon got to get back to the forest." " I Cant work in this light and soon it will be dark" "Yes your right" Basil said " sorry to keep you Sir Gustus", "It was good seeing you after all this time." Then he went back to his van and drove off down the road to the camp waving goodbyes as he passed by. Just as Basil Burton's vehicle disappeared down the road Gustus heard a woman's voice. ."Would you like a cuppa Mr John". He looked up from his work and saw her. She was a rather attractive middle aged woman well looked after for her years and rather dumpy he thought. "That's good of you" he replied.

"Well wash up in our scullery and come through" she said.

Gustus hadn't been called John since his art school days and he wasn't one to refuse the offer of a cup of tea. Working with turpentine all day made one dryer. He followed her across the road to the cottage and through a side door. Once inside he saw the deep stone sink and the bar of soap and washed his hands thoroughly.

"Come on through" she said. The main lounge was well furnished the walls were papered a pretty floral pattern and the furnishings were red sofa and armchairs.

"I'm Rose Sherwood "she said,"my husbands at work he's a foreman for the estate" .Gustus smiled.

She said " I was told you'd be coming and saw you talking to Regs grandson earlier then that gypsy man" . She wore a bright red pinafore which covered the front of her buxom figure. No doubt she had a good living thought Gustus.

She called through the back," Jane "come in now leave the pony I am cooking biscuits and we've got a visitor" " Yes Mum" a child's voice called back.

Gustus looked around the room he saw the dark black iron range smelt the sweet aroma of the biscuits then heard the kettle whistle.

She said "OK OK im coming" "That's right Mr John sir" "Please make yourself at home". "There's some magazines there if you like to read".

Gustus looked on the table where there were coloured magazines of The town and country and similar ilk. Not to Gustu liking he preferred the more saucy ones which his friends brought him from the continent with photos of nude women in provocative sexy positions

. "Here you are" she said as she laid the tray on the well varnished table. She said "There's sugar and milk there help yourself Sir".

"Thank you" he said,the biscuits were large and wholesome. Gustus loved the set of crockery cups, saucers and jugs all blue willow patterned the lady has taste he thought.

"So you have just recently moved in " he asked "Yes its really lovely here and such a good view across the heath can see why she called it heather view" she said.

Gustu replied "yes its certainly very charming and the brickworks so very unusual." She answered him "Must have cost her a fortune to have built, mind you she not short of a few bob" she laughed. "Yes" Gustus replied "he ha".

"She said "Lady Wimborne has quite a few properties around but none like this" " we lucky as we were offered one of those workers cottages just up the hill, but im glad my husband chose to rent this one, she said "I guess its because of his position with her and him being in charge like" .

"Yes you could be right" Gustus replied.

Just then a young girl entered the room. " This is my daughter Jane she s just 8 and been playing in the back on the swing." " Jane this is Mr Augustus John the artist he's painting the cottage for the Lady Wimborne". The girl nodded and said " hello mister" John acknowledged her "Hello Miss". Rosemary gestured to her "Sit down Jane, here's a drink of orange juice" she handed her a glass. "Thank you mum "she said and smiled.

Gustus enjoyed the biscuits and soon had eaten four of these rather large wheat delicacies. "Your a good cook" he said. She replied "Years of Practice and thank you" she said.

Gustus heard the ticking of the clock on the wall he noticed its rich wooden construction. Then suddenly there was a loud cuckoo, cuckoo, sound as a wee wooden imitation bird flew swiftly out of then back into the clock. "That's lovely" Gustus said.

"Yes my husband bought me that as anniversary present was expensive I expect". Gustus nodded in agreement.

Then there was the noise of a rumbling heavy vehicle passing by outside and Gustus saw it through the large bay windows. "That will be the gypsies going down to the site next to Regs place, they all work on the clay pits and brickyards" she said."They are good workers and no trouble".

Gustus smiled.

As he sat there he thought to himself that perhaps Mrs Archer rather fancied her position in the community a lot. Then he turned to her and said "Thanks for the tea and biscuits Mrs Sherwood". "Oh that's fine just call me Rosemary" she said "your more than welcome."

"I must be off now though Rosemary""as Dorelia will wonder what's keeping me and the lights getting poorer now to paint" "Thanks for your hospitality."

"Yes that's good" she said,"don't forget Mr John anytime your this way drop in, my hubby would love to see you too."

"Thank you" Gustus said. then he said goodbye to the girl who was reading a young girls book and he went back to the clearing. Gustus packed up and left the Mannings heath road, perhaps for the last time.

CHAPTER SEVENTEEN

TRAVELLING DAYS

Romany Genes
I went to visit Romany Genes
I chanced upon the Gypsy queens
with vardos there all on display
and heathers bound for chavvys play

The Gypsy king was true to form
with tales of old and wheels all worn
the road was hard when folks were true
to Gypsy lore and common dues
the customs then were fit for a king
with common rights and everything

The fairground charms with darts and lace
with fortunes told to bright ones face
the walks to market village greens
the wayward men and words obscene
the dancing gal's with tops that spun
castanets and lewdly folki songs they sung

The ponies free to graze the moors
with tattooed bridles and woolly shawls
the yarns that Horace Cooper told
folks said that he had a heart of gold

They burnt their homes as they died
and jumped the brooms each happy groom and bride
the heaths were rich in rabbits stews with
ferreting for each boy blue

Romany Genes are rich in law
with roads a winding and Vardos tall
with lamps that shone with brass so clean
like Gypsy's eyes at fall and halloween

Ray Wills

Over the days, weeks, months and years from the day I received the ALMANAC and I had read its many pages its chapters and its Sayings. I had gained knowledge and insight into my peoples history, culture and destiny from its wonders to its grace. I read about the nails of the cross of the Lord as well its its civilizations. I discovered many truths as well as myths. Our people were there when the Pyramids were built. They were there in the time of the great wars and the Christian pilgrimages.

In more recent times in Europe and in the quarrying of stone among the creative masons of Portland Purbeck stone. Stones which was used for the building of the modern London in times of Christopher Wren as well as major stone structures throughout the world.

Reading the book I learnt about astrology and astronomy the creation of mankind and nature and its importance the health well being. The importance of clean air and water and the natural remedies of herbs.

I discovered the third eye and its link with intuitions and understandings the abilities to read the mind the palm and the cards. I discovered many Christian truths as well as the way that modern religious cults abused Christianity to create false religious belief which led to wars and slavery. How church leaders created great plantations where our people were in slavery long before the German Hitler period.

I discovered the way that acts of countries such as England created land reforms which controlled people and kept them in semi slavery. I read about the planets the sun and the moon. I learnt about the destinies of our people and their wanderings. Herein I chanced upon the original Sanskrit script of the ancients along with the wording of original manuscripts of the Egyptians and before. The doctrines of the masters and creators of gypsy stories, myths and fantasies. The fairground shows and its peoples the early potters, brick makers and workers of iron and tin.

Over the future I would have so many of these travels all of which were lessons in time and place.

Here are just a few of them.

NOMADS OF REDSKIN VILLAGE

The Wild West Show

The big top came to Bournemouth in Queen Victoria reign
there were coppers on the doorstep then
in the British sun and rain
Buffalo Bills wild west show
the posters did proclaim
the queues were kind of long then
and all the children came

There was Bat Masterson with wild Bill Hickock
and little ole Calamity Jane
there were horses ridden bareback
Indians shooting bows and arrows aimed
with wagons trains and buck boards
cowboys suits and fancy clothes
the stagecoach rode into town
Poole buses were packed
with lasso's a swirling round and round
and gold bullion in the sacks

The greatest marksmen came from that far away land
and their shooting galleries were so grand
with cow-pokes hollering out loud
and randy ladies fees
the music it was loud then
and the band it sure did play
like moonlight in Kentucky many miles away
the songs of Dixie
battle hymns of the republic
I can hear those songs even today

The stars and stripes were living there
on the flags atop the hill
where the ladies all came to visit
whilst the lords bowed to the thrills

for the wild west show was vibrant
like the buckskins that were worn

The big top offered sanctuary
from the days of foolish wars
when gentleman wore bowlers
an the poor man caps n all
their six guns were afireing
freely there
whilst the crowds all did applause
in the days of Queen and country
where the gentleman always kept his word

Ray Wills

I was awoken from my sleep by lots of noise like horses galloping and the sounds of cheering.I stepped down from the wagon and looked around and couldnt believe what i was seeing. It was like a scene just out of a cowboy and indian western film. I saw a large entourage of cowboys and indians in their hundreds. All led by what looked like the familiar figure school boy famous cowboy buffalo man Buffalo Bill Cody. He was on horseback at the front and held the large union jack flag in his right hand. Then i realised this was the famous wild west circus show here from the states. The area was common land here which i knew as Mitcham near London. As they rode through i coud see in the distance by the woodland there was a gypsy camp. Consisting of many gypsy benders and tents and with gypsy folk going about their daily life. Some were sat around the yog eating and drinking. Whilst others were involved in weaving baskets cutting wood pegs or other activities. The smoke from their yog camp fire seemed to attract the attention of the entourage. As they passed the camp they stopped and looked intently. The red indians in partucular were very inquisitive and i could hear their talking amongst themselves. Then it dawned on me that they were comparing the gypsy similarities in life style to their own, with their campfires and teepee and nomadic outdoor lives . I heard them questioning Bill Cody who obviously himself recognised the amazing similarities between the Gypsies and the north American Indians, particularly the Sioux and the Iroquois tribes. He was answering all their many barrage of questions and he explained to the indians as best he could that these were gypsies. The entourage stopped, dismounted and went across to the gypsy site and i watched as they all talked to the gypsies. Then they were invited into the camp and sat with them and the gypsies shared the yog and food with them. They stayed there for the rest of the day and then when Bill bill said its time to go it was agreed that some of the indians woud stay behind for a while at the camp and catch up later.

A local Gypsy remembers. " I was always told when i asked why was it called redskin village","i was told it was because my grandparents were travellers or from travelling families and there skin was as dark as an Indians" "I was also shown photos of my great grandparents and the type of clothes they wore looked a lot like the clothes you would expect to see North American Indians wearing, every one was related."

Gypsies had originally come in their hundreds to this area from many miles around for the Mitcham Fair, local work and due to the closeness of Epsom and the Derby. They camped on the common and soon there was more than 200 Gypsies living here. Many of whom had settled here after they were persuaded to leave the common and settle on the wasteland that was Rock Terrace which became known as Redskin Village.

Some 230 Travellers were here living in vans and tents and to this day the area still has a high Romany population. This was a very large encampment mainly due to its proximity to Epsom Downs and also to the popular Mitchum Fair. It was also a centre of herb production, particularly lavender which required a large temporary workforce. To cut the flowers when they bloomed ready for distilling into lavender oil. As well as working on the harvesting, the local Gypsy Travellers would also buy bunches of lavender to sell on the streets of London. The local Romany women would often be seen going from to door to door with arm baskets laden with clothes pegs and wooden flowers. Selling items made by the men folk. These items helped to supplement the family income during the winter months until it was time to return to the countryside for the annual round of farm work. Local Gypsy men were common on the streets providing services to the locals with their grinding barrows. With sharpening of scissors, saws and knives, whilst others mended chairs. Often they were seen sitting on the pavement kerbs weaving new cane seats.

Very many old Mitchum families claim Romany ancestry and it's still not that unusual to see lads riding hefty piebald horses bareback through the traffic! They appeared to be all travelling families with skin as dark as an Indians. For folks remarked that they all wore what looked a lot like the clothes you would expect to see North American Indians wearing. It was said that everyone here was related to one another and all the grown ups were known as Aunt or Uncle. Amongst them were the Sparrowhawks, Harriett Smith the herbalist and the Bushaways.

Mrs Nellie Sparrowhawk was a familiar figure on the streets of Mitchum, where she worked as a lavender seller and with her friend Black dot Sarah Smith. Many of the Sparrowhawks family were dark skinned. They still have a scrap yard in Mitchum common to this day. Many of these families *were* flower sellers, wreath makers. horse dealers or fairground people. Such as the *Bowers, Matthews, Lees, Stanley's, Cooper, Bateman, Gray's, Ayres, James, Does, Penfolds Bushaways, Sparrowhawks, and Clarks.*

Many settled more or less permanently at the area's several caravan yards or the terraced houses of 'Redskin Village.' They worked in the local mills or pickled lavender in the local lavender fields nearby and made artificial wooden flowers. Mitcham lavender was world famous and was sold by Gypsies at fair time. Lavendar had become very popular amongst the aristocracy. Queen Victoria used lavendar flowers throughout her reign. Redskin Village survival is in part down to the four Lords of the Manor of Mitchum, who couldn't decide exactly which bit of the common belonged to who, and so the Enclosure Act came and went without touching Mitchum. Though it's long-term survival is thanks to Colonel George Parker Bidder QC a local philanthropist, who in 1891, had the Metropolitans Commons (Mitchum)Act passed through Parliament So preserving the common from development indefinitely.

As I reflected on this. I walked back to the edge of the heath and there beneath the trees was the vardo dream wagon. I was glad to see it and made my way into it once again.

THE FLOWER GIRLS

Flower girls dreams

You l see them there on Saturdays
outside the towns great store
with their baskets full of daffodils
roses by the score

Their braided hair and darker looks
with dresses oh so gay
from heather sweet terrains they came
to wile the hours away

Their dialects course with melodies
though their words were plain
they spoke in Romini dialect their journeys here from Poole
they promised wealth good health and more to people passing
by
with smiles to warrant fortunes gain
with wisdom in their eyes

From their homes of vardos on the heaths
and songs of yesterdays
where accordions played those songs of love
with rabbits in the hay

With ponies small and dog packs calls
where heathers sweetly laid
amongst their hills where myxomatosis killed
the food of yesterday

Ray Wills

Such Majesty

We tied and tethered all our ponies, cobs
with wagons standing by
next to alders winds and bracken
whilst we drank within the kings Arms
on the alder hills of wallis downs

All the heavy iron rings
were fastened to the walls of our abode
where the wind blew over the bracken
where the sisters Talbot built the village
and the dwellings
for the poor downtrodden masses

In the time of John Augustus
in the days of Cornelia Guest

Where the heather blessed the commons
and the Gypsies rode the lanes
all encampments on the common
rich in stories true in faith
all the chavvies running free

All the wisdom of the yog fires
all the virtues of the tribe.
Ayres and Sherwood's,
Cole's and Stanley's.
Jeff's and Coopers
blessed the bride

Sprigs of heather for your luck dear
off to Woolworth s for to see
the dolphins ride upon the Poole quayside
where the ships rode out to sea

> All bound for to gain the fortunes
> rich in bounty
> in another time
> such majesty.

Ray Wills

The Town was extra busy this cold December morning, the seasonal sales were attracting shoppers out looking for last minute Christmas gifts. There had been heavy rain the night before and much of the towns square was now under a few inches of water. No doubt also partly due to the underground springs here, it being part of the mouth of the Bourne. But fortunately the trolley buses were still running. I noticed it wasn't 10 yet by the towns small clock and the Gypsy flower girls were here in force. All bunched up together by the seat obviously to keep warm all overlooking the pleasure gardens. With their winter floral Christmas door sprays wreaths and assorted large baskets. I recognised the usual mature Gypsy regulars from Christchurch, Kinson and the heaths of Turbary commons and heavenly bottom campsite. With their good dark looks, their braided dark hair and large flamboyant hats. All holding tightly onto their their deep cane baskets. They were members of the Whites,Crutchers, Pidgleys, Stanley's,Bonds, Johnston's and the Jeff's. I noticed gypsy Queen Mary Bond she often travelled into Bournemouth with her friend Tilly Johnson selling lucky heather and charms in the square. I recognised many others of the Gypsy woman like those from the Jeff's family who travelled to Bournemouth from Christchurch every Tuesday, Thursday and Saturday, with their baskets full to the brim. To sell their flowers in the town centre which they called Bourne. Along with the younger youthful pretty and slim Gypsy girls with their cotton dresses. All of them looking cold in the winter sunlight and shuffling their feet to keep warm. I heard their course Gypsy tongues and the unmistakable "yes sir" "yes madam." When addressing the rich estate ladies and gents. All of whom, were no doubt out, doing their last minute Christmas shopping. I smiled and thought to myself, nothing changes. The road traffic was heavy, circuiting the clock with folks hurrying by or rushing across the square to the stores. The Christmas tree was prominent there in the centre of the square and still was lit by fancy lights. Then i saw the copper making his way over, oh dear he looks serious i thought, no doubt after traders hawkers licences or certification. I looked towards and furtively back to where the flower girls were, but fortunately they were nowhere to be seen.

As I stood there my mind went back to when the young Betsy White was barely 10 years old when her father George had passed away. Leaving the family with no income. Betsys mother chose Betsy to go into Bournemouth Square to sell bunches of white daisies. The first day Betsy went there she sold every bunch. As a result her Mother(Louisa) instructed her to carry on doing this every day. Family legend has it that the Bournemouth Gentry purchased her flowers from her because she was so pretty. It wasn't too long then that her other sisters and cousins followed suit. So the Bournemouth Flower girls were born. Betsy was the longest flower seller amongst all of her relations and the best known flower seller of all her family.

I wondered how many years had they left here before they too would be lost to the town centre like all of its character. I made my way through the crowds. Hurrying past the girl begging for pennies and the violinist on the corner with his hat for change and his scrawled words on cardboard of "War Veteran please assist".

I was to return here many times over the years. I thought of the time I was to visit here in the mid 90s it was very much different then with the pedestrianisation which I was involved in for the council.

My mind went back to a really hot summers day when the sun was at its highest in a lovely clear blue sky. The pleasure gardens in the town centre always were well cared for by the councils nursery staff. The sets of flower beds amongst the green lawns and public walkways were so pretty. Crowds of people were passing through the gardens walk as was usual that holiday time. Mainly elderly folks out enjoying the delights of the town. All on their way to and from the towns beaches and its picture houses, hotels and restaurants. I stood in the middle area of the gardens then flanked by its green lawns and overlooked by the bandstand. Where the towns famous symphony orchestra was known to play. Along with the salvation army. I looked around at the swing boats and then assisted the rows of eager customers of all ages onto them. Whilst taking their payments from their hands and then they climbed on board the boats. I was now busy recording their numbers present in the book on the table. There were a few of us here then mainly volunteers. The object was to raise moneys for the charity for the aged. It was quite an occasion, the boats were very colourful, wooden and painted yellow with fancy gypsy style scriptural art work. It was strange that i had been chosen to be involved on this challenge. The aim was to be in the Guinness book of records for the most people to ride swingboats in one day. Bearing in mind that my relatives once were the main swingboats gypsy owners for the great fairgrounds. Fairgrounds which travelled throughout the land and also assembled at the great race courses such as at Epsom and at the sea side resorts at Brighton and on Blackpool's famous Sands. Where they were all consulted by royalty for their wisdom and fortune telling duckerin skills.

At the end of the busy day I made my way back to the car park where my vardo dream wagon was and I climbed aboard to lay on my bed and once again to reflect on all things.

Crowds were gathered here in the old white Pelhams house in Millhams lane Kinson. Samuel Sherwood thought it was best to speak out now he had been quiet far too long. He took a deep breath then said "So how was it that all those years ago, just a few gypsy families had paid out a substantial amount to buy this land on Turbary common." "And yet now we are here generations later." "having it taken away from us under our very noses." "And there's nowt we can do about it" .

There was silence in the hall because they all knew sadly that he was right of course. He thought to himself the Gorgas had once again, stripped us of our rightful inheritance. After all wasn't this land our peoples from the earlier Domesday s. From the time they we had first entered England in the 11th century. And not as their gorgas historians had continually told us that we had arrived here in the fifteenth century. Then a young Johnson spoke up. "Hey wasn't this land ours any-ways Mush." "Till they enclosed it all into strips to make moneys." "On top of that our people had worked the farmlands and many of us were given land in respect of our reliability." Then a women's voice spoke out. "Yes he's right" said Susan Miller. Susan's family had businesses in Newtown for many years and she knew her family history. She raised her voice so she could be heard above the noisy gathering."Of course Michaels right." she said. "This was our land as rights and they took it and then sold it back to us." "Now they're taken it back again under their gorga law." "All them lords and ladies had handshakes with us regularly on a number of good deals in those early days." "A handshake deal was a man's word and honour then." "Of course" she said. "There was nothing in writing, it wasn't the way back in those earlier simple uncomplicated times."

Then a commanding figure a tall dark haired traveller at the rear of the hall spoke. "So what we going to do about it Mush." Nigel Stanley was a well known respected member of the group who knew his roots and wanted action. His question aimed directly at Samuel. Up till now he had been quiet, but now he was more concerned with the facts before them. . Samuel recognised Nigel as a member of the oldest grouping of travellers in the locality. With a history going way back to the new forest days. Samuel knew Nigel could be trouble if this wasn't in some ways resolved. Nigel spoke. "Mountains of household and garden junk have been piling up for years at one of the sites turning it into an eyesore and were getting the blame." Samuel spoke out. "These few local residents of Bournemouth and Poole have always bemoaned the mess left behind by travellers setting up camp in public parks and beauty spots for sometime that's a fact." "But the problem is far from one-sided its not as simple as that." Then Basil Burton the former campsite warden at the Mannings site spoke up then in defence of the gypsies on Mannings heath." I showed the Echo paper reporter people around the site in Mannings Heath site recently." he said. " I pointed to all the items of rubbish which didn't belong to the Gypsies." "It was local people who were dumping their household rubbish on the site and the gypsies took the blame." he said ."It happens all the time" . "The dam press and their lies". "Gypsies would not burn down their own amenities either." "That would be daft." "Gypsies would not ever think about setting fire to the roofs. For roof tiles are worth a lot of money and if so they would have surely they would have taken the tiles off before." Just then another gypsy spoke up. I recognised him as from the Phillips family. H said "My family spent years defending our right to graze our stock on turbary common under the Domesday book and now the authorities do this" . "How come lord Wimborne can sell off 200 acres of commons land to Poole council". "Land we lived on for years legally bought and he can make such a profit running into millions of pounds". "Why even the house of Lords in London kicked up a real ruction about it". "Apparently there was a right goings on with them and uproar in that place." "Travellers had always been allowed to pitch on this corner of the heath with the express permission of Lady Wimborne" "Provided they behaved and kept a tidy site". "There was never any trouble until Poole Council bought the heath "Then them Police got warrants and they turfed us all off, men, women n children". "Its a big injustice our folk been there for years". "Generations of our people lived there "." Its only thanks for the likes of Gypsy king Tom Jonell along with lay preacher Ronald Vivian fought for the Gypsies case",. "Now they plan to evict us all and to build some 1400 houses I am told"."Here's the funny thing" he smiled," You l never guess what they are going to call it a park after the water tower, yeh Tower Park, what a mockery".

After the public gathering at Pelhams hall ended and well before everyone left. I slipped out the main entrance and walked outside of the great house and into the large expanse of its great estate off of Millhams lane. The trees there were rich with leaves and full of birds song. There under the great oak was the little vardo dream wagon, it looked so fragile there and always without a horse. I made my way into its small room and stretched out on the bed. My mind was full of questions along with many disappointments. I thought of all those years of our people all their journeys they had taken and then to come to this great disappointment. It made me feel very sad to see what it had come to. As I lay back on the bed I then fell into a deep sleep.

I was awoken by the movement of the wagons wheels and the crack of a whip. I sat up and loo ked out of the small window and saw the glass frontage of busy street shops. In their reflection I saw the driver of my vardo. He was a middle aged gypsy, rather shabbily dressed but with a large hat on his head. In one of his hands he held the reins of the grand white horse who drove the vardo wagon and in the other a large whip. He swung the whip above him I heard it crack menacingly in the night air light. I heard him swear loudly in a Romani tongue. As he drove on into the night through the street lit town and I fell back into sleep and dreamt.

Dorset Steam Fair

The old fair is here each year
Upon the downs with fun and beer
the oil doth smell and tracks of mud
where cars are parked upon the meadows so green
whilst the carousels play to delight the scene

The crowds flock here again this year
to buy the goods or storm the gears
there's gypsy folks and travellers tales
amidst smoky air and diesel smells
There's a big machine to roll and ride
across this Dorset countryside
where zunners run and play and stare
at all those folks there at the fair

With marquee tents with music rock
stalls for to sell and gears to lock
with amusements rich amidst fields of green
bikers parades and beauty gypsy queens

Crowds of folk flock here each year
to mingle and enjoy the spirit here
with the hills so steep and views so grand
the steam fair spreads itself across this land

Ray Wills

The road to Blandford was extra busy today as i made my way by car to the Dorset Steam Fair. Eventually i pulled in to a space in the temporary car park site. I managed to park the car within hundreds of others on the steep grass hill overlooking the fair. As i made my way down i noticed the abundance of Steam engines which had tore up much of the tracks creating huge stretches of brown clay mud lined avenues. The smoke and the fumes from them were filling the air now as many of them rolled their way over the downs. The music from the variety of organ machines was really loud. Then i entered the main thoroughfare with its large marquee tents. These tents choke full of rowdy drinkers being entertained by folky and country musicians. I walked through the crowds. Mingling amongst all the bargain hunters busy exploring and handling items on display. To the right was the unmistakable fairground booths, the carousels,swish backs and swing boats and bumper cars. Whilst Diana Turner was in her fortune teller booth busy dukkerin. Nearby was the leather jacketed greasers with their proud motor bikes all neatly parked up. Many of them I recognised as the chapter from Birmingham double zero club. I stopped to have a chat with Tony a large figure of a man with long shoulder length hair. Tony just came as he did every year. "This is our day" he said "We look forward to this every year". "Love the atmosphere here and the gypsy people are so easy going". "Many of our chapters come here today like we do every year". "Though must admit we have come across a few awkward ones over the years".I asked "Do you go to the fruit picking at Evesham . He said "Nah not our scene, we love the music here the beer and the fairground makes a great day out". "Yes your so right" I said" Pity they don't have the tulip festivals in brum like they used to those were also great days out"." Yeh its all changed these days" he said "Lot your people are stopped on the road" "I've seen it" he said "its a real shame." I agreed and told him about the groups like kushti bok who were campaigning for gypsy rights still. "Yes ive heard of some these" he said. "I think there was an artist who campaigned for gypsies for years" " but obviously he's long gone." he said. I said "You mean Augustus we called him Sir Gustus" "Yeh that's him"he said. "He sure did paint some wonderful people"" Yes" I said "But his real love was painting gypsies". "Yes he must been a real gentleman" he said.

CHAPTER EIGHTEEN

REFLECTIONS

Travellers Lament

She took a reading he worked the forge
She collected flowers she mixed the herbs
He bred the horses and mules a few
full of birdsong on the heaths of Poole

He worked the fairgrounds she flew the darts
He rode the cars starlight in the dark
She cooked the stew he told the tales
the land was rich wagons and tails

He shook the hands and bartered deals
She picked the fruit turn turn turn wagon wheels
they used the stopping places and atchen tans
He told the stories he was the man
wise old ways gypsy man

She stood for Munnings pictured frame
Stanley's, Lees, Coopers,James the same

She dressed in skirts and wore gay bright rings
He wore the waistcoat boxed the sports of kings
She fashioned flowers paper crepe
He worked with clay gravel and bricks

She sang the songs of Caroline Hughes
He wrote the stories like Dominic Reeves
She modelled for John at Alderney
He built the cottages Lady Wimborne free

She danced at pubs in forest glades
he collected iron scrap
She was Queen thousands at her grave

He was a scholar poet bard
She was a countess he played the cards
She was a sweetheart of Byron too
He was a wanderer traveller from Poole

She was a coal merchant he was a king
She was a Crutcher he was a White
where miners did sing.

She was a dreamer he was a priest
She saved lives he saved souls to teach
She was a beauty and he was a rogue
She was a prophet indisposed

He was a fool
they rode their wagons
through the streets of Poole

Ray Wills

I felt her soft hand on my shoulder and her soft feminine voice sweetly spoke directly to me."Your friends are outside she said " Theyve been asking for you,they thought i had abducted you". I felt as if I'd been awoken from a deep sleep. Then it all came back to me i remembered all the travels. I looked up at her, her dark eyes looking concerningly at me. Madam Rosa smiled and said "You have travelled well my Raymond" . "Our peoples have a long history dont they". "And now you have the knowledge," "Use it wisely my friend". I smiled and said "thanks Madam" .Then i left the booth and stepped out into the daylight. I looked around and saw all my young mates were all outside skylarking around as usual. The tallest boy amongst them Jimmy Dominey spoke "youv been a long time mush", "We thought she had taken you in the back for a bit of hows your father mush". They all laughed at this. "No I should be so lucky " I said. "I had a wonderful experience though il tell you about it sometime". They were all quick to respond with a barrage of questions. "What did she tell you, it must have been good duckerin "." Did she tell you anything we should know about" ."Did she tell you youl make a kings ransom at the races"," or be chased by the gavvers" ,"And how many women youl have in your long life" they giggled.Then they all followed me out into the night and into the future. No he thought to himself She had told me that "These were just fanciful dreams". "Dreams and hopes like men have all had from the beginings of time itself". She had said "remember always that your still just a gypsy youl never be anything else". "Youl never be a gorgar never be recognised as anything else". He remembered what they had told him over his years of travelling in his or her time vardo dream wagon. Hadnt Augustus John or Sir Gustus himself with all his fancy high pulletting and freedom loving ways.He with all his grand pictures there in all the great galleries of the world. Yet still he was a gorga. He tried to be one of us old Gustus but that woud never be. He was just after all just a traveling gorga nothing else. None of his dreams or ways would ever make him a Gypsy traveller. Like the fairground lady Madame Rosa had said i myself like him would always be a dreamer. I turned to look for my dreams but they were just memories of the past and the future or were they. I looked for it in the Almanac and yes i still had it.Yes i still had the book and it still moved me I still read out the lines of bravery and freedom of my people and I knew that i was still after all a royal king, yes a king of the road.

Since our people first roamed the lands of the world it seems we were cursed. We were treated with utter contempt, discrimination and often ran out of the town or country. It was a common misconception that we were child stealer's, thieves and a dirty race and that always we left our rubbish behind everywhere we went. Vast numbers of our folk were imprisoned or sent on slave trade ships to new found land Canada or transported to the new world plantations in America, or in prisons settlements like Botany bay in Australia. Many of our people were imprisoned there or elsewhere and even hung. Most for minor offences such as poaching rabbits or horse theft or even for just being a Gypsy. Most of such crimes were committed out of pure necessity to survive, We were chased through countries even for having no original homeland. Unlike others like the Jews. Yet we had much in common with that nation of peoples we had our faith and our regimes. We celebrated religiously and we had strong moral ethics and all manner of cleanliness. Our dogs were not permitted in our caravans. We were one with nature yet always roaming and travelling the roads Our home was wherever we laid our heads. In the early days our folk slept in man made benders. Then we had wagons with horses yes we always had a special way with horses. Then we had Vardos and in recent years trailers. Initially we lived in the forests and woodlands of England. This was our main habitat a sheltered leafy sanctuary. It was often told in folk lore that it was our people who saved the ponies from drowning in the wash during the time of the Spanish Armada. We cared for them and bred them and they became our means of livelihood and transport. Our people had many skills in ironmongery, tin smithery, pottery, brick making and our women were great soothsayers, fortune tellers/ dukkerin as well as basket makers herbalists and flower sellers. We were said to be a very intuitive peoples. Working in the fayres markets and in the town centre selling flowers such as at Bournemouth. Working on the lavender fields and in the mills. We worked the land for centuries collecting fruit and hops for the farmers and rich landowners. They knew they could rely on us. We were good reliable workers returning each year to the farms and fayres. Our men were great with the horse providing farrier and black smithery skills. We were great at bartering prices often at a time when the common handshake of a gentle man's agreement was binding. We were permitted to live on the land during this time and even strips of land were provided to us by the landowners. We were of many different tribes in many areas of the kingdom. We tended mainly to keep to our part of the country though we attended great gatherings each year where we met up with members of other Gypsy traveller tribes. We exchanged goods and stories and bartered whilst our young people met up with cousins and those of the same age. Many young people met sweethearts in this way and in future times married in a local church or jumped the broomstick. The churches of Catholicism were often critical of our people as we tended not to take to their services preferring a more simple Christianity. We lived within tribes with familiar Gypsy traveller names such as Smiths,Blacks,Sherwood's,Stanley's,Coopers,Lees,James,Woods.

Many of our men folk dressed majestically in fancy waistcoats sporting bold tattoos and our women folk too with braided hair and gold ear rings and long floral dresses. Most of our people had some particular skill in entertainment often many were fiddlers,dancers,singers and musicians. There were many who were storytellers and our elders encouraged such talk or says around the yog campfires in the evenings. We worked the travelling fairgrounds which were seasonal around the country with their boxing booths. Our young men came from a long ancestry in pugilism and through centuries many became world champions of boxing. Often as a direct result of being on these travelling boxing booths. The fairgrounds and the circuses provided seasonal work with their many stalls, darts,coconuts shies bumping cars swish back rides, swing boats and the ever popular fortune telling booths.

    There was a period when artists flocked to our encampments and at our gatherings to paint our people in what was known as the romantic period and many great pictures are still shown in the art galleries of the world today.

    Of course some of us don't like to be called Gypsies these days preferring to be called travellers. But even this term is seen in a bad light by many of the non Gypsy settled folk. Lots of our folk have settled over the year and their modern day off springs live on large council estates many them bought up in the thatcher right to buy years or have got on , with their own houses. Of course many them are not aware they have gypsy blood roots ancestry or even if they are they prefer not to say so. Many of them are ashamed of their gypsy origins Mainly caused by the discrimination that still exists out there today With some travellers who leave a mess when they vacate a field or invade an area camping on a children's play area or recreation ground..Often with there being no temporary transit sites so called atchen tans or stopping places available. As there was in the past when families travelled down for to attend a family funeral christening or wedding.

Some of us bought the land or came to mutual arrangement with the farmer/landowner as a trade for services. Much of these transactions were by a Gentleman agreement. Often consisting of no more than a customary handshakes between the gentleman farmer and the gentleman Gypsy. So often these strips of land were passed on from one generation of traveller to the next over many decades or even centuries.

We were particularly loyal to these farmers who depended upon our labour each season for collection of crops and fruit picking.

There were rumours of government proposals to halt our wanderlust with its life of using stopping places. Which we had used throughout history so many with courtesy of local landowners and of course throughout the farmers fruit and crop picking seasons. There was always talk of the gorgas lawmakers and their powers. Their objective was to persuade us to give up our travelling ways and become settled into permanent housing in the settled community like all the gorgas. To pay rent,rates for water and use of the land. To become employed in what they called regular employment, which usually meant unskilled factory work. We lived in communities known as encampments or camps. These all were very different in size and numbers with extremely unusual names. Names which included Cuckoo bottom, Frying pan and Heavenly bottom. Our community of Travellers despite our inbuilt wanderlust had been loyal to our country. With many being active in the armed services through numerous wars and campaigns. We are travelling folk.

I was awoken after a restless night by the sound of knocking on the vardo door which was unusual for it had never happened before. There outside stood the driver of my vardo. He was taller than I thought and looked a lot older. "I want to talk with you Mush" he said in a deep Dorset accent. He said"As you know mush ive driven this wagon for many years past, present and future". I nodded. "Well mush" he said" im as you know getting on in years". He continued to talk "As you have discovered all our histories through your many travels". "I feel the time is right for me to hand over to you".

"What do you mean" I asked. "Well" he said "there's many a young gypsy traveller who would gain much benefit from travelling as you have don't you agree".

I nodded and said "yes I guess so".

"Well" he said" I feel its time I retired and gave you the reins" "So here's I am and the Horse is still a good olé boy and im sure you l both get on well."

" Hang on a minute" I said "now let me get this right. your going to leave me to the wagon" "to be its rider into the past and future".

He said "Yes me acker youv got the gist of it". "Your more than capable now and there's lots of youngsters gypsy travellers who would benefit from the experiences you v had" "don't you agree".

"Have you discussed this with anyone" I asked "such as madame Rosa"for instance".

"Oh yes I have" he said "and she's all for it she said you'd be ideal for the job with all your experience".

"So how will you cope, what will you do in your retirement" I asked. "Well I thought long and hard on this" he said "and I made the decision".

"So what's that I said. "Well im going to move to Bere Regis village" he said "Got me an apartment there in West street". "Its a dwelling especially within a gathering of retired writers, artists and musicians". "It was set up by Cyril Wood of Bournemouth Symphony orchestra some years ago."

. "That sounds good" I said. "Though I didn't know you had artistic leanings".

"Why yes I play the harp and piano accordion" he said "plus I write a little mostly poetry".

Sounds great" I said. "Well You never know" he said "I may find myself some widow lady in the village who will take pity on me". I laughed. "Well I wish you the best" I said.

We shook hands and I watched as he walked away down the hill.

So it was, that I stepped up to the mark. I sat on the front of the vardo dream wagon holding the reins of the lovely white horse and we rode together out into the future.

GLOSSARY

PEOPLE

SIR GUSTUS - The Artist Augustus John
RAYMOND
CAROLINE HUGHES - Gypsy
JOHN TURNER - Gypsy
MACEY CASTLE
REG ROGERS BRICKMAKER - Mannings heath
ALICE ROGERS
TONY ROGERS
WILLIAM bill ROGERS
MARY FANCEY - Dairy Maid Bere Regis
JEAN HOPE - Gypsy
BRITTANICA KEATS - Gypsy
SAMSON STANLEY - Gypsy
SANKEY WARD - manager of clay pits
FRED BARTLETT - Gypsy fairground proprietor
MUNNINGS /MONEY BAGS - Painter
TED SHERWOOD GYPSY - Boxer
MADAM ROSEA GYPSY   Fortune teller Blackpool sands
SAMUEL SHERWOOD - GYPSY
THE LAMB GYPSY SISTERS - Dancers
BASIL BURTON - Gypsy Warden Canford Heath gypsy council site
PRINCE MICHAEL - Royal leader of pilgrimage

ANNABELLA - High Priestess at Little Egypt
MATTHIAS COOPER
JOHN WHITE BOSVILLE
LAURA KNIGHT
THE AMEY BROTHERS
ROSEMARY SHERWOOD
SAMPSON STANLEY
THE DREAM VARDO DRIVER
PETER LOVELL - Publican The rising Sun
CHARLIE NEWMAN - Landlord of the square and compass
PRINCE ANDREW

PLACES

ST HUBERTS - St Huberts church Corfe Mullen

ST ANDREWS - St Andrews church Kinson

MILLHAMS WHITE HOUSE - Millhams lane Kinson

THE MILLHAMS MEAD - Kinson

THE VENTURE - Children's Adventure playground West Howe

THE SQUARE - Bournemouth

WOODBURY FAIR - Bere Regis

DORSET STEAM FAIR - Blandford Dorset

THE SANDS - Blackpool

POOLE FAIR

POOLE QUAY

THE PLEASURE GARDENS - Bournemouth Dorset

CANFORD ENCAMPMENT - Poole Dorset

THE SQUARE AND COMPASS PUB - Portland

NEW ENGLAND - Gypsy campsite Kinson Bournemouth

HEAVENLY BOTTOM - Gypsy campsite Canford heath Poole

THE MANNINGS HOUSE - Smallholding Mannings heath Poole

THE MANNINGS CAMP - Gypsy campsite Mannings heath Poole

CUCKOO BOTTOM - Gypsy campsite Canford Heath Poole

KEMP WELCH - school Parkstone Poole

PELHAMS - community centre Kinson Bournemouth

REDSKIN VILLAGE

HEAVENLY BOTTOM - Gypsy campsite Poole

TALBOT VILLAGE - Bournemouth

CANFORD MANOR
PELHAMS HOUSE - Kinson
THE WHITE HOUSE - Kinson
MILLHAMS MEAD - Kinson
LITTLE EGYPT - gypsy encampment
EPSOM

RECOMMENDED READING SOURCES AND RESOURCES

The Gypsies - Charles Leland 1882

Gypsies of New Forest-Henry E Gibbins (1909)

"Gypsies, Their Life, Lore, and Legends - Printed in Great Britain by Latimer Trend & Co Ltd Plymouth Konrad Bercovici

Stewing The Pateran- The Gypsies of Thorney Hill – John Pateman "Gypsies of Britain - Brian Vesey Fitzgerald) Pompeu Fabra University

Gypsy Folk Tales- Francis Hindes Groome, [1899], at sacred-texts.com

Gypsies of the Heath - 'Romany Rawnie' aka Betty Gillington published by Elkin Mathews 1916

My friends the Gypsies - Lawrence Bohme

The Forest Gypsies - H Leksa Manus's - The Roads of the Roma

The Gypsy's Parson; His Experiences and Adventures (1915).The Rev. George Hall's

Charles Godfrey Leland's "professor" in teaching Leyland the Romany language -Journal of the Gypsy Lore Society-

Wanderers in the New Forest - Juliette de Baraicli Levy (1974). Juliette De Bairacli levy, Paris (1953

Queen Victoria's Sketchbook-M Warner-Macmillan, London (1979).

The Project Gutenberg E Book of The New Forest-Elizabeth Godfrey (1912)

Romany and Traveler Family History Society-rtfhs.org.uk

An Artist's Life - Sir Alfred Munnings- (London 1950).

Romanies In Dorset and Hampshire- Sue Cole.

An Artist's Life (London 1950)-Sir Alfred Munnings

Where The River Bends- Raymond Wills - Lulu.com

THE ENGLISH GYPSIES -THE PENNY MAGAZINE -January 1838

GYPSIES IN ENGLISH HISTORY – DAVID CREASEY CREDITON- DEVON- April 1840

The Traveller times magazine

AUGUSTUS JOHN The new Biography Michael Holroyd, Head of Zeus Limited.

GYPSY TRAVELLERS IN NINETEEN CENTURY SOCIETY By DAVID MAYALL Cambridge University Press

Village life and labour Raphael Samuel 1975 Routledge

Stopping Places – Simon Evans, published by Hertfordshire Press 1999.

Memories of the undefeated Bare knuckle champion of Great Britain and Northern Ireland. Bartley Gorman. Cox and Wyman.

GYPSY TALES By RAY WILLS Amazon 2020

THE GYPSY CAMP By RAY WILLS Amazon

WHERE THE RIVER BENDS By RAY WILLS Lulu

Printed in Great Britain
by Amazon